GENEROSITY

GENEROSITY

Stephen Slaughter

The Book Guild Ltd
Sussex, England

First published in Great Britain in 2002 by
The Book Guild Ltd
25 High Street
Lewes, East Sussex
BN7 2LU

Typesetting in Times by
SetSystems Ltd, Saffron Walden, Essex

Printed in Great Britain by
Bookcraft (Bath) Ltd, Avon

A catalogue record for this book is
available from the British Library

ISBN 1 85776 607 5

For my grandparents

CONTENTS

LOYALTY

As he had finished the novel that was going to change the world everything had altered. There hadn't been time to check it for mistakes before he'd had to run. Now, with the storm subsiding, he had to get it sorted, see what it was and what it meant to him. His soul had gone into it and he was having a hard lesson seeing it as a piece of wreckage to cling to. All his observations, insights and knowledge had been distilled into a prose that could wake a generation just in time. He had joked that she would have to watch out for it wouldn't be long before masses of those girls that fell for brilliant authors came knocking on his door. They had worked alongside each other, she on her drawings, he on his manuscript. Many evenings he had sat for her as she outlined the details of him that interested her. For his encouragement and approval she returned new slants on words and fresh ideas for him to torture. It had been a passionate and productive time for both of them. Or so he had thought, now she had left him everything was upside down.

There was a knock on his door. Sophie put her head into the room.

'Do you need the bathroom, I'm going to have a bath in a minute?'

'Sounds like a great idea, I could do with a bath, I'll be with you in a tick.'

Sophie wasn't quite his type but if she wanted to bathe with him how could he turn her down.

'No, I'm having the bath on my own, creep!'

People often call names using buzzwords rather than honest observation. It's a device to claim credibility, a game of tag, file and forget to be ready to shout the next body down as quick as possible. If you're not in someone's face you're nowhere. It's a shallow game anyone can join in.

'Witch! You're just frightened you couldn't control yourself up close to a body like mine!'

He listened to her raucous cackling as she went down the stairs.

At first he had been going to hang himself. He still had the rope, he'd actually made it himself from a long ball of string. It was in the box, along with his manuscript. The two things were bound like a dressing around his wound. At once the manuscript gave him both a reason for living and for not living anymore. His whole life had tangled into it, it was his truth, his dream. The ingredients of the dream had turned out to be poison, though and it was no good to him or anyone. And the rope too had this double image of either binding or freeing, he could either hang on or not. Before he could go any further he had to sort it out. So he had set aside the coming weekend to read his novel. Many months of toil had gone into the making of it, moments snatched after working hard all day to keep body and soul together. He retrieved it from the bottom of the big cardboard box he'd thrown his few belongings into when he'd fled the sinking ship. It was nice to have some solid proof of his efforts to hold in his hands.

It was early on a Friday night, a free weekend ahead. There was a time when he'd have been ringing round his mates to find out what was happening, where everybody was drinking, where the parties were. Those days were gone. Now instead The Nature of Things would be revealed in his story. At once he wanted it read already, done with, and at the same time he wanted to pitch it into oblivion. Yet he couldn't do that in case it wasn't true, in case it wasn't an accurate portrayal. He would have a cup of coffee and then deal with it. He went downstairs to make some.

4

The aroma of cooking greeted him as he entered the kitchen. The person responsible, Graham, was everything Colin despised, an ignorant journalist who sported a moustache and made pretentious conversation. Saying he was ignorant wasn't the whole truth, he'd been to university, got his degree and doctorate so he ought to know something. Colin often wondered how so many people drifted through life unaware of and untroubled by hardship. Compounding the injuries of an unfair universe, Graham also had a very attractive girlfriend. The stupidest thing was that he wasn't interested in her. He really wanted a platonic relationship, somebody to look good on his arm while the poor girl just wanted to be shagged silly. Of course, that's being simplistic, she wanted Graham because he treated her so well. He was too polite to be honest and, besides, he genuinely wanted friends, so he kept building her up and making her feel good and then at the last minute would shut her out. He didn't deserve the love she wanted to give him. She spent tearful hours on the phone to Sophie trying to unravel her confusion.

Colin never let the slightest hint of his disgust show. Despite his sins, Graham was after all a likeable chap, forever outgoing if a bit wishy-washy. He was one of those people who profess to being socialist, never seeming to be aware the label covers a million shades from the palest yellow to the bloodiest red and that he could be more specific. Colin had learned to avoid politics, he knew his own mind and left it at that. Very few people he met even knew why Right and Left were so described. He meditated on his lot to fall among such weirdos.

There had always been weirdos. In one house he lived in, for instance, there was a chap who was a vigorous cook after the Jackson Pollock school who felt colour and character needed to be added liberally to what he considered was a cold and sterile kitchen and took offence at being told the encrustations he left over the cooker, walls and floor on each visit were not really wanted. Graham agreed it was only sociable to be clean and tidy. He cooked irritatingly well and offered to share with Colin the chili he was preparing for himself. Karen, his gorgeous girlfriend, was moving house tonight into a nurses' home just round the corner. She had declined Graham's assistance for some reason and so he was spending the evening in. Although Colin was less than devotional about chili, it was free and so he didn't need persuading. He even nipped round to the off-licence to get some wine to go with it. The result was that after eating he spent most of the evening drinking and watching television with Graham.

Malcolm, another member of the household, was at some sort of works do, a retirement party or something. Sophie was in and out of the house all night, clomping up and down the stairs, first on her own, then with her girlfriends, giggling like schoolchildren, and then finally with Stuart, arguing noisily. Graham couldn't take Sophie seriously, referring to her as 'Airhead,' a favourite adjective of his. Colin liked her a lot but felt her choice of friends, especially Stuart, was suspect. Malcolm came in late and spent a long time on the phone assuring Mary, his girlfriend, he wasn't drunk and then slurring dreadfully. Love! Colin was sure that what had passed between Caroline and himself had never been quite so sickly. Then again he remembered a few occasions many moons ago that had been a bit stupid, especially in the light of recent events. He had known the girl all his life only to find he hadn't known her at all. He wasn't sure if he knew anything anymore. Many times in his day-to-day life now he found his concentration wandering like an idle schoolboy, kicking old situations around in his head as if they were tin cans that needed realigning in some clearer, finer order of things.

Too tired to stay up, Colin left Graham and Malcolm watching the midnight movie and went back to his room. His unread novel stared up at him accusingly, shaming him. Yes, yes, he would deal with it, soon. Once in bed he turned the stereo off and realised Sophie and Stuart were hard at it in her room next to his, just feet away. Irritated, he wished he'd left the stereo playing. He couldn't turn it back on now. He pulled the duvet up around his head and plunged into sleep only to be hauled back into consciousness some-time later by banging and shouting. Another argument and Sophie was chucking Stuart out for some reason, he didn't catch the details. He drifted back to sleep again.

Next day he was up bright and early and wandered downstairs in the quiet house to find Sophie crying in the kitchen.

'What's up, Doc?'

'What do you think, creep?'

'There's no need to be like that!'

'Don't ask stupid questions then!'

'I was only trying to be friendly, no need to bite my head off.'

Busy wiping her face with tissue Sophie didn't respond. Colin was suddenly annoyed with her for not taking his interest kindly.

'I could say I wasn't too pleased at being woken up at one o'clock in the morning by people shouting at the tops of their voices.'

The girl fled upstairs.

7

'Stupid cow!'

He sat at the table with his breakfast and read the previous day's papers. After eating he took the unfinished crossword back to bed. During a struggle with some cryptic clues he fell asleep and woke a lot later, hot and sweaty. The weekend wasn't working out quite as planned, not just for him but for others also. Karen hadn't moved after all, she'd had to do another shift, covering for somebody who'd gone sick. She was going to have to move later, after she'd had some sleep.

Colin had a pile of laundry that needed doing and he wanted to get to the laundrette early on before queues developed. He tramped over there with his bags. Just by the door a young girl with long blonde, hair came out and brushed past him on her way to the sweetshop. Briefly their eyes met and seemed to snag. It seemed like the moment took ages or perhaps it was just Eternity doing a somersault. Inside the laundrette he found a machine free and started bundling his clothes in when suddenly she was back and all around there seemed to be activity, a million things going on. She wore a pop group's T-shirt, Deep Sleep, a band Colin liked. It gave him an opening and they started talking, which seemed to slow things down a bit. Even so the wash was done before he'd really got started and was dried in moments no matter how slowly he put the coins in. His charred emotions dragged his impulses, it had only ever been Caroline before and now he felt deceitful and torn. He wished he could wipe away the past. He wanted to impress this new girl and thought about mentioning his novel but decided against it. It might have helped if he'd had plenty of money, was rich enough to take off on any whim or even go for a drink. In the end, being pretty boracic, he just packed up his stuff to go home, hating himself and everything else all the while. The rope would have cured these ills. His clothes were clean but his soul was dirty. He hoped he would see her again and have a better chance.

Back home he was having some tea and constructing a shopping list from the gaps in his cupboard when Sophie appeared. She was always flying in or out. He greeted her with a smile.

'You must have smelt the kettle boil!'

'Has Stuart rung?'

'No,' Colin answered, only for Sophie to swear.

'What are you doing?' she asked when she'd calmed down.

'Shopping list. A single man's work is never done!'

In a cackling, witchlike way Sophie's laugh could be quite pretty but Colin was wounded by the implication she made with it.

'Where is everybody?'

'Graham's helping Karen move, she had to do a double shift last night.'

'Oh God, she's a fool moving nearer. I've told her to move away, leave him alone, give herself a chance to meet other people, there's plenty out there. She just won't listen and she's only going to get upset again. She drives me up the wall. God knows what she sees in him.'

Colin wanted to make a pertinent comment about a certain other person and struggled to find the right phrasing but before he could the time had passed and she was gone, thumping up the stairs to her room.

After he'd returned from the supermarket with all his purchases and put them away, putting away half the biscuits at the same time, he took a cup of tea up to his room and got the weight off his feet. He'd had a busy day and once he sat down he felt tired and sleepy. As he drifted off towards a short nap a vision of his situation horrified him. He was falling apart and had a million things to do. The determination to sort himself out before Death had a chance to catch him off guard took on a dreadful overwhelming urgency. He really had to get himself in order. When he came to, all the anxiety was gone and he stared out of the window for ages before he picked up his manuscript and began to read.

It was a great feeling. Here he was with his own work, his very own story. He was pleased with the size and weight of the volume. It was a snappy piece about humans, the environment and the end of the world. It was very true and tackled all the world's problems head on, a sort of ecological romance with a sad ending. Many times in the past few years he'd imagined the thrill of being published, he'd imagined the world finally taking notice of such an important message and also he'd imagined being fabulously wealthy. Great rivers of dreams, dreamt each night he'd spent stitching his work together, flowing endlessly down to a wonderful, clean sea.

Reading was another matter. After a while he was glad he hadn't mentioned it to anybody and especially glad he hadn't mentioned it to that girl. Caroline knew about it but he'd never allowed her to see his efforts. Now they looked so poor, so feeble in the cold light of day. Disappointment and misery invaded his body. The line, 'Where hope once was, now all aches end,' from the poem described himself perfectly. His thoughts, so vivid in his imagination, when condemned to paper drearily smothered the pages. Writing had been the most absorbing and interesting, the most complete an occupation he'd ever had and now there was nothing left. The rope would have prevented this misery but he was thankful he had not left such an inappropriate epitaph. His small room, once comforting in many little details, now just intensified his inadequacy. Feeling cold and dejected, he decided to have a bath. Down in the bathroom he was surprised to find Sophie's things in a heap in the middle of the floor. He checked with the others, went back upstairs and knocked on her door.

'Can you clear your stuff out of the bathroom please? I'm going to have a bath.'

'Oh no you can't, I'm going to have one, I just checked with everybody.'

'Not with me.'

'I didn't know you were in, there wasn't any noise, your stereo wasn't on.'

Just because he had a ghetto blaster didn't mean to say it had to be on all the time.

'Well I was and I want a bath!'

'It's too late, I'm having one. I've got to go out tonight.'

It would take ages to reheat the water.

'You had a bath last night!'

'So?'

She was defiant. That was it, she had done it this time, the girl really was the limit.

'Never mind.'

Back in his room he collected up his woollens and took them down to the kitchen. Luckily there was nobody using the sink. By the time he had washed and rinsed all his hand washing thoroughly the hot water was running cold. He was very pleased to have got one of his chores out of the way like that. Malcolm was engrossed in the football and was shouting encouragement to his team who seemed to be a bit deaf. Once established in front of the TV he rarely moved. 'Sedentary' was a word invented just to describe him. Graham was out somewhere, probably still assisting Karen. Colin climbed upstairs and resumed his reading. As the hours went by the disappointment he had felt before came back just as strong. He had wasted a perfectly good weekend to do this, to ruin his confidence. He made some coffee and sat drinking it in his room but felt too oppressed, he had to escape.

Outside was fog everywhere. He wanted to run and run, away from everything again but there was no direction to go in. Chilly questions swirled around him. He felt he was utterly alone in the world. If he could just have a sign that he wasn't, that there was somebody just for him. Magically a breath of air cleared the fog directly in front of him and revealed Karen who was unloading things from her car. While a misty mugger poured icy water down his spine and pulled out his entrails and threw them away, he exchanged greetings.

'How's it going?'

'Nearly done now.'

'Graham helping?'

'Yes, he's gone to get a Chinese.'

'Great! Oh well, see you.'

Colin hadn't stopped walking all the while although he'd slowed and turned to be polite. Now continuing on his way, he imagined all sorts of situations. He couldn't believe what had happened. One second he was asking for somebody and next second almost out of nowhere somebody appeared. Surely it was just coincidence. Karen off all people. What if it wasn't coincidence? He would never find out, not while he knew Graham anyway. He should have asked if she wanted any help. She probably thought he was a right selfish so-and-so for not giving her a hand when he could have so easily. If only it could have been that girl from the laundrette. His mind now spinning fervently, he walked round the block and returned home. Tomorrow he would finish reading his story and decide what to do about it.

On Sunday morning he woke from a complicated dream about symbolism. The seconds were out and Jung and Freud were in the ring and Jung was beating the crap out of Freud. Difficult to get an angle on really. He used to write his dreams down but they got progressively more complicated the more he remembered and he ended up taking longer and longer to record them. Why he couldn't just dream about shagging all the time, that's what he wanted to know, he'd surely sleep a lot better then. He got up, washed, shaved, dressed, made some breakfast and went to buy a paper.

It was a bright, sunny morning and as he made his way he saw the girl from the laundrette. She was stood reading adverts outside the shop. People were walking in and out past her and soon he would do the same. His mind seemed to fill up with the whole of the previous night's fog and he couldn't think of a single thing to say. He croaked the feeblest of greetings and faltered on his way past her but she didn't look up and he had to go inside and buy a paper. It would have been just too corny to stand behind her and read the ads as well. He wished the world would give him a break, make things a bit easier for him. He trudged homeward. Before long his mind cleared miraculously and he thought of a brilliant thing to say. He turned round to go back but the girl had vanished. At the house he had a quick look through the paper and decided that the world was just past caring about. Throwing the paper down, he returned to his manuscript. A few hours later he finished reading it. It wasn't going to change his life in the way he had hoped, it wasn't going to shake the world. He wasn't as dejected about it as he had been the night before but it was an enormous disappointment. He very badly wanted a change in his poor existence. He needed something to take him out of himself.

Sitting there looking blankly out of the window at the bricks of the next door house it suddenly dawned on him that if he hurried he was still in time for the Sunday lunchtime session. Putting his preoccupations aside for a while, he stirred himself and set off out. At the pub there were a lot of people about. He saw the girl from the laundrette again. She was hanging on the arm of a dirty, ugly man with a bad complexion. Perhaps it was just as well she hadn't heard him earlier on if she was into people like that. Eagerly he tried to master the art of conviviality and with the help of quite a few pints by closing time was in a very good humour. As the pub doors closed and everybody left, a sense of hollowness reeled him homeward more directly than he should have liked. His bed engulfed him and he spent the rest of the day asleep.

It was late Sunday evening when he woke and he was cross with himself. The weekend hadn't gone at all right. His mouth was dry and his head was thumping and a journey to the kitchen to make some tea was well in order. The house was quiet, the others had retired. Very sensible people, like riveters on holiday, not riveting but interesting in their own ways. Mind you, he shouldn't be so sarcastic. What did he, the great novelist have to offer? A story with as much impact as a call for intelligent government. Collecting his novel from his room, he took it and his tea and sat in the living room. Maybe there was something he could do with it, other than destroy it. Flicking through, he read bits at random. Really it needed completely rewriting, which would take a lot of work and time, maybe another two years. Dispirited, he threw it down and poured himself more tea. Having thought everybody was home already, the sudden opening of the front door surprised him. Sophie entered the room and sat down on the sofa next to him.

'Hi!'

'Good weekend?'

'Not particularly.'

'Nor me.'

'Do you want some tea?'

'No, ta.'

'I need it, I had a few beers at lunchtime.'

He fetched her a jovial grin, finished the cup and poured another.

'Stuart and I have split up.'

'Are you pleased?'

'What do you think?'

'I'd say you were better off!'

'He isn't all bad.'

'Matter of opinion.'

There was a pause. Colin worried for a moment in case Sophie would burst into tears was relieved she didn't.

'What's that?' she pointed to the sheaf of papers.

'A manuscript.'

'What?'

'A story.'

'Who's is it?'

'Mine.'

'Yours!'

'Yes, mine.'

'What do you mean? It's something you've written? You've written a story!'

Colin was a bit irritated with her incredulity.

'Well, I can read and write as it happens!'

'You mean it's really yours, not somebody else's?'

'Yes, it's really mine. Anyway, perhaps I ought to be getting to bed.'

'Can I read it?'

'No.'

'Why not? Surely you wrote it for people to read.'

'Yes I did but it isn't any good.'

'That's why you're fed up?'

'You could say!'

'I didn't think you were the sort of person to do anything creative.'

'Why not?'

'I don't know. You just seem, well you never seem to do anything except buy music and get drunk at the weekend.'

'Isn't that what everybody does?'

'Not exactly.'

'I didn't realise there was an element of critical perception inside that pretty head of yours.'

'Don't be sarcastic, everybody categorises everybody else.'

'Sorry, I suppose we all make mistakes every now and then.'

'Yes.' There was a long pause.

'Oh well, I suppose I had better get off to bed, up early in the morning and all that! I'll see you tomorrow.'

Before he managed to get up Sophie spoke again.

'I was thinking, I've got some tickets to a Deep Sleep concert on Friday night. I had been going to go with Stuart but he's not going now. I don't know if you'd like to go?'

'I'd love to! They're my favourite band!'

'Do you really think I'm pretty?'

'As witches go.'

The silence this time became filled with the most fascinating activity.

As Colin lay in bed he reviewed the weekend. It seemed he had found a different perspective already. There was no hiding place from change. There were some compensations in the turmoil. He listened to the shallow breathing at his side and wondered if he would ever really know this new person. As for Caroline, she could go hang. That his novel wouldn't make the impact he had hoped it would only showed what a dreamer he really was. The truth will always get you in the end.

AMBITION

Arthur was working his way, door by door, down Pit Street without any luck at all. It was nearly 4.30 on a typically awful Thursday afternoon and he hadn't sold anything all week. His third week without a penny. That was not counting the four policies he had from the first week. Rob, his supervisor, had done those for him. They'd been Rob's cronies with renewals but he'd put Arthur's name on them to encourage him. It was a gesture to help a new boy starting out. Not so much a boy, at 31 it was a mid-career change for him. The way things were going it wasn't looking like the best move he'd made although those four policies had provided a decent income for the first week. Now toiling down the cold, dirty street he wished he had some more warm leads to call on.

If he could just get somebody on their own to do a presentation he wouldn't have minded. Each time he found a prospect and got started a host of sceptical co-workers appeared and poured scorn. He was offering a good scheme as well, he really believed in it. Still the words, 'Not interested,' echoed in his ears again and again. He chanted the refrain, 'A quitter never wins and a winner don't never quit,' a snatch of song from a favourite musician. It was as much as he could do to boost his flagging confidence. Passing a cafe, the urge to go in and sit down swept over him but he really should resist. Cold, tired and hungry, a vision of the tea he could have filled his mind. It was hard putting work first with such tempting images to compete with. He could almost feel the coffee cup in front of him and almost hear the food being prepared for him. He knew that if he sat in the warm atmosphere even for a few minutes he would feel sleepy and his head would slip forward and the rest of the working day would disappear. Going in would be a betrayal, not only to Claire, whom he was depending on while he got on his feet in this new career, but also of himself. He could see the red faced proprietor's smile as he said, 'Thank you,' and pocketed the change.

Coming upon an old and grimy doorway he wondered if he should try it. A suspicion he'd not seen it before made him wonder how much of one's surroundings, even the most familiar, does one never notice? There was some sort of sign over the door but it was too dirty to read. He remembered his training sessions and the importance of being methodical, he was supposed to go from door to door and never miss one out. Well, he'd been doing that, he'd hit the biggest place in town first thing, was rejected there and had been turned down in every place since then. 'Not interested!' 'Got some already!' 'Don't want any!' He'd heard all the answers. It was his rebuttals he had to brush up on. He tried to remember at least one.

'Now isn't it true that if you broke your leg it would hurt?' 'Yes.'

'Now isn't it also true that if you had a broken leg you couldn't work?' 'Yes.'

'Isn't it true we could all use a thousand pounds a week?' 'Yes.'

'Well sign this, you blasted moron!'

It was no good, that wasn't the proper formula. He would have to go over them again tonight. He should use the exact words they had given him or he risked failure. Failure, what was that? 'Oh well, nothing ventured, nothing gained.' He straightened himself up, put a friendly smile on his face and pushed open the door.

Inside he found himself going down steps. The air carried traces of strange smells, like toast burning or something cooking. A draught caught him and he coughed and coughed. Giving up smoking should really be his top priority but then what pleasures would he have? When things were better he would give up. When . . . it didn't bear thinking about.

'Jeez, this place is warm!' he swore and pulling out a handkerchief mopped a couple of trickles already forming on his forehead. There was a slightly unnerving ancientness about the place. It was like going down the worn steps into the dungeons of all the castles he'd been to as a child. The gently spiralling steps appeared to be cut from the rock before Time began. A flutter of apprehension circled his stomach looking for somewhere to land. After an age of going down and round that was getting him dizzy he pushed through a heavy door and came out into a massive cavern.

The noise, heat and above all smell of this place convinced him it was a chemical plant. It was a giant operation and he was surprised he hadn't known of it before. There were ladders, pipes, huge valves and antiquated machinery everywhere. Lines of gigantic vats receded into the distance. The noise was deafening, he could hardly hear himself think except to mention something needed oiling badly. It sounded almost like screams, as if thousands of terrified voices were wailing in agony but it was probably just the decrepit machinery. High above him the workers, some of the ugliest people he had ever seen, were prodding and stirring away at the stuff in the vats, whatever it was. His observations were interrupted by a deep booming voice.

'Oi, what are you doing?'

Brandishing a large stick and bearing down on him was a vast, cloaked figure with a ruddy face and a ferocious expression. He began interrogating Arthur.

'What do you think you are doing here?'

To say Arthur was indignant at having, as he would

put it, some geezer prodding him with a great big stick would risk understatement. His pleasure wasn't increased to note that the thing had spikes on it as well which was surely against all health and safety regulations. It made him wonder who this geezer thought he was.

'Hey, be careful, who do you think you are talking to?' he demanded.

'Only the worst come here!'

The red man glowered at him ominously and prodded him again.

'Watch it, that's enough of that!' and with an angry reaction Arthur grabbed the stick and took it off his inquisitor even though he seemed twice Arthur's size.

The element of surprise worked in his favour and he yanked the stick and turned it round and quite accidently jabbed his opponent who yelped and spluttered.

'My arm look what you've done!'

Arthur saw his chance.

'Now you see if you had some accident insurance you could have claimed for that.'

He pointed to the wound and gave back the trident. Opening his presentation folder and with his pen already in his hand he continued his banter.

'An accident at work like that would have paid you, let's see . . .'

He flicked over the pages of his folder.

'Well, let's say you lost the use of your arm you could have had four hundred a month for almost a year. Of course the more units you buy the higher the income if you have an accident. Nobody likes to admit it but accidents do happen, as you well know.'

'What?' the prospect spluttered. 'You come into my domain, stab me in the arm and . . .'

Arthur felt he had some advantage although he was

24

momentarily taken aback by the prospect's stentorian bellow.

'Beadle! Edmonds!'

Although he hadn't given the full and proper presentation Arthur knew that the moment was critical and decided to go for the close.

'So may I include you?'

He clicked his pen meaningfully. Now he should have been giving, 'The Strong Forceful Look,' and in order to do this he looked up to a pair of eyes that seemed infinitely deep and desolate but his glasses were too misty. As he fumbled with his spectacles and handkerchief the prospect's two attendants came scuttling up.

'Did you call us, your Lordship?'

'Yes of course.'

Not having seen or heard the two new arrivals Arthur was delighted with his success and quickly replaced his glasses and began filling in the form. His pen flew over the paper ticking boxes and writing in details.

'Naturally you'll want full cover and maximum units. Tell me which bank do you use?'

'Banks! The man pesters me about insurance and banks! Do you think I've got time for parlour games? What sort of ordeal is this?'

'You don't deal with banks, a building society is it? That's fine.'

Arthur continued talking as he wrote.

'Halifax is it? That's the biggest.'

'Halifax! Halifax! Didn't you see the sign on the door?'

'Local branch is it?'

Like a brain surgeon with a blunderbuss he blew away the poisonous rage rapidly infecting the prospect.

'I suppose you could say this was a local branch, a lot of people find it very easy to drop in.'

He was pleased with this reply. Disappointingly, he didn't get many opportunities to impress people with his wit and he was happy that his true, urbane character should come to the fore once in a while. Swelling a little with vanity, he sank into unhealthy reverie.

'Account number?' queried Arthur, still busily writing.

His client, who hadn't had a decent sleep in Ages, was entranced by pleasing images and was drooling.

'Fee, fie, fo, fum, I smell the souls of hopeless ones.'

'3–5–0–1–0–1, fine. It's funny I have a mnemonic to remember mine. Now if you'd just like to sign here.'

He proffered his presentation folder with the filled in form ready. Suddenly exasperated at being dragged from his delicious mental meanderings the client lunged toward Arthur to shake him but his arm caught the sharp corner of the folder and dark blood splashed everywhere.

He yelled, 'Ow! Get out before I . . .' and dropping his trident to clutch his arm he did a little dance of pain. 'Just get out!'

A bit taken aback, Arthur tried to compose himself and noticed there was in fact a mark on the dotted line, in the commotion he obviously hadn't noticed the geezer sign.

'That'll do!' he cried, well pleased. He tore off the top two copies and handing over the client's copy said, 'This is yours.'

He made to shake his new client's hand but noticing prodigious nails changed his mind.

'Nice doing business with you!' Now I must dash.'

'Beadle, Edmonds, you smelly heaps of rag, get rid of him!'

Always prepared to look for the best in others, Arthur put his client's agitation down to a bad day and having to work in such a hot and noisy environment.

'Jesus, it's hot in here!' he exclaimed.

Emitting an hideous wail, Arthur's customer fled.

'Not that name . . . no!'

Without ceremony the two lackeys marched him out of the building. It wasn't until he was halfway up the stairs that Arthur remembered the most important thing, money.

'Hey!'

With amazing effort he managed to stop and loose himself from his two escorts' hold.

'It's no good, I've got to have the first instalment, I have to have some money.'

Saying that, he began to make his way back down the stairs.

'No!' yelled the guards together as they caught him.

After a quick conference one of them dashed off down a passage Arthur hadn't noticed was there. A few moments later the chap returned and thrust a couple of coins in his hand and then the two propelled him up and out through the door back into the dark, cold street outside. It had been a long day but he felt a lot better about it now. Most of all he just wanted to go home and relax. Zipping up his presentation folder he set off back to his car. As he made his way, chinking the coins in his pocket, he couldn't help wondering if his luck was at long last changing.

Beadle and Edmonds were finding out theirs wasn't.

'YOU DID WHAT?'

'We gave him a couple of coins and chucked him out . . .'

Edmonds faltered as he bore the brunt of a terrible roar that shook everything to the foundations. Raging and cursing, the loud one stormed up and down smashing anything in his way with his trident.

'You gave him some money! You blithering idiots! First you tell me the guard wasn't feeling very well, of course he wasn't feeling well, he's not supposed to feel well, no one here feels well! Then you tell me you gave some money to an insurance salesman who should never have been here in the first place. What did you give him?'

'Two gold coins.'

If exasperation could have been calibrated on a scale the gauge would have exploded at exactly that moment.

'TWO GOLD COINS!'

Horrible boils appeared all over the two abject bodies, their beards caught fire and they shrank to less than half size before the one with the power calmed down and restored them back to normal. It was all very well having fun but he had things to do. Cursing them in every language, he considered the situation.

'Oh for the pennies of Charon, why can't I have obedient people? All the incredible things I could achieve with a few even half-decent staff but instead I'm stuck here having to put up with miserable, incompetent specimens like YOU!'

Of course he knew exactly why he couldn't have anyone good but that never stopped him cursing.

'And, by the way, where did those coins come from? I know you just found them, you thieving, good for nothing heaps of dung. The question is where?'

Their memories were too frightened to function. He would have liked to put a stop to their squirming little existences altogether but in fact they were useful as any he had to work with and he didn't have time to keep training new staff.

'I ought to make you burn.'

'We thought you'd be pleased!'

The rounder one's pathetic outburst made him laugh.

'Perhaps you did but each of those piles of money and valuables is a payment belonging to someone. None of them must be touched, ever! Do you understand?'

To ensure they did he caught them each with a small prong of his trident and held them over a convenient fire.

'How could anyone trust me if I lost things all the time. I won't cheat anyone, especially those already determined on eternal torment. Turned from His face they must know the exact cost of their forfeit to the last coin.'

Desperately and with arms and legs flailing, they both pleaded total comprehension. He swung them back over firm ground and shook them off the spikes.

'Also those coins may have gone out of circulation centuries ago and what's that chap going to think when he finds ancient coins in his pocket?'

'Don't know sir,' they answered, still clutching their sides.

'The point I'm trying to make is that it would be best if he lost and forgot about them fairly quickly.'

They agreed utterly.

'So what are you going to do about it?'

They looked at him blankly.

'Us sir?'

'YES, YOU!'

'Get the coins back sir!'

'Exactly! But remember this place is secret. If people

found out it was real they might start behaving properly and where would that leave us?'

'Somewhere else, sir?'

'No, you stupid idiot, Cerberus help me!'

He clasped his head in irritation and counted ten before explaining.

'No, what I mean is we'd still be here but I'd have nothing to burn, isn't that so?'

They nodded.

'And where would I be if I couldn't keep the Damned Fires burning?'

'Don't know, sir.'

'Out of a job, that's where I'd be and then I'd want to burn you wouldn't I?'

They nodded their terrified heads again.

'And would you like that?' They shook their heads violently.

'So what can't we have?'

They looked pretty vacant.

'By the waters of the Styx, what is it that we don't want?'

'We don't want any dinner sir?'

Such an unexpected reply made their inquisitor laugh a second time.

'Oh poor Beadle, are you hungry?'

'Yes, sir!'

'Well you'd better get used to it! No, what we don't want is anybody upstairs knowing we're here. That's why when you go you must stay invisible. Got that? And you have to act soon and hope this chap will forget or think he's been dreaming. So!'

Blankness again filled their faces.

'What are you waiting for?'

They scuttled off, bickering.

'That's the last time I listen to you!'

'What do you mean, it was your idea!'

'It never was!'

'I could never think of anything as stupid as that!'

'What does he mean, "Upstairs?"'

'You know, "Upstairs!"'

'No I don't, anyway how do we make ourselves invisible?'

'We get cloaks, apparently they do the trick.'

'How do you know that?'

'I don't know!'

Once he got home Arthur had a hot bath that was so comfortable he dozed off in it and he ended up having to wash in nearly cold water. All the same for some reason he was in a good mood and as he dressed he made singing noises. Claire dashed his high spirits on a stony old promise.

'You remember you're taking me to the airport tomorrow?'

'Of course I remember!' exclaimed Arthur, who had completely forgotten.

He had agreed several weeks previously as she would need a lift while her car was in the garage. Inwardly Arthur cursed. He really needed to get out there straight away and sell more policies, make the best use of his enthusiasm. It was all about confidence. It was typical, just as things were going his way she dragged him down. He couldn't avoid taking her to the airport and that would be his whole day disrupted. She was holding him back, if it wasn't for her he could really get on. Maybe if he was lucky and sustained his confidence he could start properly next week.

'I wonder if I'll ever get on in this business!' he sighed meaningly.

'I hope so,' replied Claire missing his emphasis. 'You need some money.'

Bills poured in endlessly and she was sick of paying all of them. Her agreement to help him while he got on his feet in his new career was wearing a bit thin. She wouldn't have minded so much if he made an effort around the house but he just sat there reading his paper or watching the television. She wanted a proper life, doing things, going places and having fun. Also she hoped one day to have a baby. She didn't want to bring up a family on the breadline, with Arthur it was more like the crumbline. It was all right for him, time doesn't matter to men. Nothing much does. Booze, football, TV, they live in a dream. They think work is over once they leave the office and as for pain . . . well. Besides what if she met somebody else? Some rich passenger or a nice pilot. Somebody half-decent who wasn't a slob and had some money, what then? An attractive 27-year-old like her had a lot to offer the right candidate, not that Arthur ever noticed. Look at him, he always falls asleep in that chair.

Once cloaked, Beadle and Edmonds proceeded up the long spiral staircase and out through the door, now guarded and looking like an ordinary wall. This was their first assignment upstairs and being neither here nor there took them a while to get used to things. Beadle in particular found his cloak very troublesome and was always moaning that it was too small. It wasn't long before they realised they had no plan. They had no idea who Arthur was, where he lived or how to find out.

'What about the piece of paper he left?'
'What about it?'

'Blimey you're stupid! Is there any information on it?' Edmonds took it from his pocket.

'No not really, it's all about Mr Redman.'

'Who?'

'Mr Redman, that's what it says. Mr Redman, Chemical Works, The Cave, Pit Street. Hey hang on, is that the boss? I didn't know that was his name!'

'Actually I don't think it is.' Beadle's brow was furrowed while he tried unsuccessfully to remember something.

'Anyway, is there an address for the salesman?'

'No, just his agent's number.'

'Oh well, so much for that idea!'

'He's put, 'The Cave,' as Nick's address.'

'It's horrible isn't it, I don't like it. All that noise all the time and it's so hot you can't breathe!'

'And he's signed it A. Brown .'

'Hey, we could look in the phone book!'

This could have been a great idea if they'd have had a phone book or knew where to find one. Things were looking pretty bleak until they realised their situation gave them plentiful opportunities for childishness. Although neither of them had much grip on reality they found they could make people jump, knock people's hats off and all sorts of things. They got so engrossed in playing tricks on passers-by they spent all night and half the next day before remembering the mission they'd been sent on. It was long past the time they were supposed to report back. Their excuse of getting lost was not very well received and they were told in no uncertain terms that if they didn't get the job done pretty quick things would get very hot indeed for both of them.

'Damnably hot!' It was emphasised.

Being methodical and ignoring all the distractions

33

this time, they found their way to Arthur's flat by the next morning. There was nobody at home which gave them a chance to have a good look round. They were very thorough in their search but sadly for them the coins were not there.

Claire was in a foul mood. She'd had an awful flight with a plane-load of ghastly passengers and then had waited fruitlessly for nearly an hour in the freezing cold for Arthur to pick her up. There had been no answer when she had phoned the flat so she guessed he was playing his usual Sunday morning football. She went and got a cab, irritated at having to fork out money needlessly. When she got home she found the place was an absolute tip. It was the last straw. There probably wasn't time enough to detail all Arthur's shortcomings even supposing there was an adequate language. Her bags were already packed, she called another cab, left a note to say she was leaving and marched out. She was sick of always tidying up after him, sick of cooking for him and looking after him. He was just a loser.

Arthur had spent most of the football match in goal. He wasn't sure why he bothered really when he wasn't considered good enough to be let loose on the field. One day he'd tell them he was playing in attack and they'd all be surprised by his skills or, more likely, he just wouldn't bother turning up any more. At the pub later he purposely didn't get drunk because he knew he had to pick up Claire from the airport in the evening. He just had a nice quiet session, watched telly round his mate's place in the afternoon and then progressed to the airport and spent a few hours playing the computer games before making his way to the arrivals lounge. Searching the screens with growing dread he realised that he'd missed Claire's flight

34

entirely. It had come in at 10.14 in the morning and he was 12 hours late. What would she think? He knew what she would think. With a feeling like molten lead pouring through his stomach he dashed home to find his relationship torn apart.

He was sure he hadn't left the flat in such a state. He had to admit it was a bit untidy but it surely hadn't been that bad. If he had thought it would make such a difference to Claire he would have tidied it. Why hadn't he tidied it anyway? Now she was gone. He didn't know how he would manage without her. He wondered it she had found somebody else. What if she had? What was he going to do? He had been so preoccupied with his own problems and now he'd made all his problems a hundred times worse. His thoughts chased themselves round and round his head until, sometime in the morning, they were too dizzy to remain upright and they fell into a black knot and he slept.

After a night of putting the wind up a few folk out walking and feeling much better for it, Edmonds and Beadle caught up with Arthur as he began work for the week. So as not to lose him again they kept as close as possible and followed him into his first call. They were hoping for a convenient moment to confront him about the coins. Arthur had had virtually no sleep and felt like death warmed up but he was determined to make this job, his career, his priority. He had to prove he was worth something before he could put the rest of his life in order. It was no good running after Claire and begging her to come back when there was so little for her to come back to. She had been right, he had been useless but now he was determined to show her he could change, could earn a decent income and take control of his life. He had managed to escape from the dead end job he had before and this was his best chance, it was vital he didn't mess it up. Rob had already worked out a plan of action with him for the next week and he stumbled to his first call, a place with quite a few employees.

Keeping positive Arthur gave a presentation with the appearance of great confidence. Tapping his pen on the laminated sheet as he underlined the wording on the folder and fairly yelling out the spiel, he made sure he held his prospect's attention.

'This is the way to do it!' he thought to himself, 'He can't fail to sign up.'

As Arthur made a particular point halfway through the presentation the prospect looked up toward him and turned completely white. Edmonds, who noticed, turned and saw Beadle's cloak was undone and the hideous fool was standing there grinning away as plain as day. He pulled the cloak shut properly and dragged Beadle from the shop.

'We're done for now, you stupid idiot, that man saw you! You heard what the boss said, we'll fry if anybody finds out about us!'

'It's not me it's this cloak! Anyway he won't know will he!'

Once Arthur had finished the presentation the prospect agreed straight away to taking a policy and encouraged the rest of his staff to each take one as well. The poor man was still shaking when he sat down for his tea and spilled half of it before he could benefit from its soothing effects. He knew he'd been overdoing it lately and now he'd had a timely warning.

The hapless pair could not agree on the best action. Beadle wanted to go back in and Edmonds felt it wisest to wait until Arthur came out. Beadle's carelessness had made Edmonds nervous while Beadle felt Edmonds' continual harping on about trivia unjust and irritating.

'Seeing you once, people could put it down to indigestion or a trick of the light but if they keep seeing you again and again they'll get suspicious and we can't afford that.'

'I'm not going to get seen again, I'm not exactly stupid you know!' Beadle declared and set off for the shop.

Edmonds grabbed him and they ended up grappling with each other. Next thing they were being roused from their exertions by the sound of car horns blaring at them fighting on the road in full view of the rush hour traffic they were holding up.

'Now look what you've done!' yelled Beadle.

'You've really done it this time!' screamed Edmonds.

Getting up and dusting themselves off they disappeared as quickly as possible. Sulkily they waited outside awhile but Arthur had left by the back door. Suddenly sensing they'd stood too long the waiting pair rushed through the shop only to find Arthur gone. Back outside they draped themselves disconsolately over the railings as best they could although they tended to slide ever downwards. It was all very well gliding through walls and doors and all that but to keep up required immense amounts of concentration and without enthusiasm the world began to get on top of them.

'Now what?'

'It's all your fault!'

'How did I ever get into this mess?'

'Same as me, you cynically . . .'

'There he is!'

They both watched open-mouthed as their quarry drove past.

'His car! Why didn't you think of that? See, you're useless, you never think of anything.!'

'I'm useless! I like that! You keep claiming you're the one with all the brains, you should have come up with it.'

'Look, the bus!'

Seeing a bus moving off in the same direction it was the work of an instant to board it. This gave them a short but welcome opportunity to play tricks on the passengers.

With eight policies signed and in his folder Arthur considered he'd done enough for the day. He would resume his operations at the next place the following day. He really needed to see Claire. She would be staying at her sister's place. He made his way there and knocked on the door.

'What do you want?'

'Can I come in for a moment?'

She let him in automatically, before she'd even asked herself if she wanted to see him. Shrugging her shoulders, she conceded that they had to talk sooner or later.

'I'm sorry about meeting you, I got it wrong, I was at the airport for ten in the evening.'

'You're a fool!'

Then she itemised a few more of his characteristics that she had forgotten to mention before which made her feel a bit better. Arthur felt the conversation was rather one-sided but as he had come crawling to her he had to accept it. Besides, he wanted her back and he wasn't sure if she was going to come back. In an effort to impress her he showed her the policies he'd sold in the morning and explained the income he would get from them. He went on to confess his shortcomings and stressed the efforts he would make to change. Claire just sat there while he spoke. She wanted to say she'd heard enough promises in her life but she just sat quiet. She wanted him to know that a very nice, solvent gentleman had invited her out but it wasn't true. He asked her to give him another chance but she wouldn't say more than she'd think about it. Driving around later that evening, Arthur could only wonder at the mess he'd made. He'd completely ignored all the signs. Nothing got rid of his feeling of desolation and the certainty he'd lost everything. Stopping in town, he went back to the cafe. He hadn't realised how tired he felt until he sat down in the hot, steamy atmosphere.

Beadle and Edmonds were wailing fit to burst. Their mission had been a complete failure. They hadn't got the coins, they had lost Arthur and now their time was up. They didn't want to go back, 'Downstairs,' at all. Suddenly a large figure wearing several overcoats and ski jackets, a huge woolly hat and thick gloves appeared before them and declared,

'I suppose if you want a job done you have to do it yourself! By the teeth of Cerberus it's cold here!'

They realised it was Nick underneath all the layers and cowered before him.

'What's the matter with you two?'

'Nothing, Sir.'

'Where are the coins then?'

'We haven't got them.'

'Where's Mr Brown?'

'We don't know, we lost him.'

'How could you lose him? Didn't anyone tell you how to get around this place? No I don't suppose anyone did. It's easy if you think about it. Come along now quick – before I freeze.'

Arthur had just finished a nice tea when a well-padded man appeared before him with two figures in tow.

'Good evening, Mr Brown, although I have to say it's a very cold one.'

It took a few seconds for Arthur to recognise Mr Redman. He began to offer his hand but remembering the nails snatched it back.

'Oh hello Mr, er, Mr . . .'

'Call me Nick,' the other replied genially. 'Actually, I'm glad I ran into you. You remember that policy I had off you the other day, well the truth is I've already got one.'

'Oh well, that's no trouble at all, er, Nick,' said Arthur.

'So I was wondering could I cancel it?'

'Yes, of course, by all means and of course you'll want your money back.'

Arthur fished around in the depths of his pocket making sure he got the right coins before pulling them out and handing them over.

'Well that's lovely, I thought it wouldn't be any trouble,' said Nick casting a glance back at his two followers.

'It was lucky I bumped into you. Anyway Mr Brown, it's been nice meeting you again. I'll let you get on, I'm sure you've got things to do. Goodbye. Come on you two, I've got some burning questions to ask you!'

After they had left Arthur felt refreshed and got up to go. His life might be a mess and in pieces all around him but he knew he was going to rebuild it. It was about time he took responsibility for himself. He'd been blaming Claire for his failures for far too long. He went to the counter to pay and spoke to the man.

'Funny name for a cafe, "The Devil's Kitchen!"'

'Oh, it's always been called that,' the red-faced proprietor answered.

He smiled a strange sort of smile as Arthur put his change in the charity box. Making his way back to his car, chinking a couple of coins he had in his pocket, he couldn't help thinking his luck was at long last changing.

GENEROSITY

Imagine a typical film introduction. The tiny planet spinning in the emptiness. A simple image that signifies a mass of complexity. It is the place in which we live and breathe, our home all around us and yet we are so familiar with this detached view we consider it our own. Clutching at falling debris we tumble towards the world and through the clouds, arriving in the harbour of a famous metropolis. We've hit town early one late winter morning. Splashing out we grab a lift with a gull and get a bird's eye view of all the city or would do if it wasn't so dark. From the docks, over the commercial centre, to the residential areas, we see the city waking up. Our gull favours a particular neighbourhood, it's fairly ordinary and decent and we land on a typical apartment block. Now, a step away from the hurly burly, we can watch the goings on. The people rushing in and out to work, shop and play never seem to stop. It's so fascinating we could sit there for weeks. Our gull, however, is not so keen and flies off on his travels in search of food with a parting discharge. Below, a girl just leaving the building for work felt this particular morning was not going her way. With the obvious curse she dashed back to her apartment to clean off the mess. A few seconds later our heroine was bent over her sink sloshing shampoo and water about. As bathrooms go hers was roomy and neat and smelt of roses, her favourite fragrance. A modest chenille mat draped over the side of the bath was blush pink, the only strong colour in the cream and white room. Above the sink a tall mirror glared at her. The sparse clutter of bottles and jars was all female. She obviously lived alone to a decent standard. After the third rinse her hair felt clean. There was no time to dry so she rushed straight off. Miraculously, then her journey flowed. She landed on the subway platform just as the doors of the

45

train opened right opposite. Nipping onto the carriage, the last seat was hers. Shivering because of her cold head, she cast envious glances at those girls with short hair before the carriage filled up. The doors closed and the train squealed and lurched toward the city. At the other end, expertly dodging raincoated commuters, she flew through the barriers, up the steps and into the street. Hurtling past the second-hand bookshop, she barged right into Sophie who was just coming out of the doorway.

'Sarah!'

'Sophie! How are you? I haven't seen you in ages! What are you doing round here?'

'Oooh, your hair's all wet! You must be freezing!'

'Yes I am. It needed washing,' Sarah said, catching her breath. 'What are you up to?'

'I was hoping to find something for Gordon's birthday but of course it's too early yet, they're not open. I'll have to wait. There's got to be something in one of these shops. What about you, what are you doing?'

'Going to work, the office is just round the corner.'

'Oh yes, of course. Aren't you lucky working in such an interesting area!'

From somebody who didn't have to work it wasn't the brightest observation but she was an old school friend and easy to forgive.

Sophie continued, 'Hey look, you must come and see my kittens, you'll love them! What's today? Tuesday. Why don't you come over tonight, after work?'

'Okay, yeah, that would be good!'

'Great, see you later then!'

'See you later!'

It was one of those grey mornings with a fine mist in the air. The damp chill penetrated right through, even rushing hadn't warmed her. A dew had formed on the

46

front of her coat and half had been brushed off by the collision. Looking piebald, half dewy, her coat was black and silver, the colours she wore most often. She arrived at her workplace at the same time as Mr Bashford and helped him open up. The senior of the two founders of the company, he was gendered ironically and his florid gestures laid him open to heartless mimicry behind his back. He had an irritable nature and tantrums which, although never aimed at her, strained the atmosphere and ensured a fairly quick turnover of staff. Sarah put up with it for the privilege of working for a prestigious company (and the money of course, which wasn't bad). She lived and breathed the art world which as far as she was concerned was all there was. New when she joined, the company was now getting established and doing very well.

'You're early today!' she remarked as the shutters clattered up.

He didn't usually grace them with his presence so soon in the morning. Answering her he spoke, as always, as if he would rather be using disinfectant.

'My wife couldn't sleep so I wasn't allowed to. I decided to get up and come in early for a change.'

It was as much as she'd learned about his wife in all the seven years she'd worked there.

'Is she not well?' she asked solicitously.

'I couldn't say,' he replied absently and stumped through to his office.

Obviously there was something going on but sadly for Sarah that was all she was likely to find out.

The first and most important job was caffeination and she scurried about opening a fresh pack of coffee and filling the coffee maker with water. It wasn't long before the aroma brought life to the establishment. Arriving in ones and twos, the other girls filled the air with noise and chatter. It was a reasonably busy office and Sarah kept it running smoothly. Once she hung up her coat the routine switched autopilot on and she let her mind drift back to her friend. She guessed Sophie had been out that early to drop Gordon off for work. Her husband was fairly high up in a multi-national bank and often worked criminal hours. They had plenty of money and this was some of the reason why the gaps in their acquaintance were getting longer. This morning the guilt of not having made much effort for so long had her agreeing without any hesitation to visit. It would be nice to catch up anyway. Sarah wondered how someone she used to skip with and walk arm in arm with in the playground, someone she used to tell secrets to and felt was exactly like herself turned into the Sophie she had bumped into earlier. Sophie had never put a foot wrong.

Catching her reflection in the window as she gazed out she could almost pretend the scar wasn't there and instead was an almost pretty face with its dark brown eyes and long, dark hair. At first she used to spend hours with make-up trying to hide the thing but it was still always there underneath. Nowadays she couldn't be bothered and just made the minimum effort and defied anybody who commented, not that many people did. Her job kept her too busy to worry too much. She liked her job and would probably keep at it even if she were to marry money as Sophie had. That was as likely as winning the lottery. The pressures of work put a stop to her musing and the rest of the day was spent reading the newspaper, chatting on the phone, drinking more coffee and trying to figure out how the new photocopier worked. When it was over she closed up and made her way to Sophie's place.

Sophie for her part had a very busy day. She hated early starts but needed the car and had to take Gordon in. Since her own car had been bashed there was a definite and very strong reluctance on his part to get to grips with the concept of letting her use his. She was a bit cross with him about it, they were married after all. Anyway it hadn't been her fault and besides it was no good him arguing, she had to have it as her car was still at the garage. There would be somebody to bring him back in the evening. It wasn't that he was mean. It was absurd to be so attached to these things. His stereo for instance, if anybody so much as breathed! After dropping him off she needed shops. It was funny bumping into Sarah like that. She was a serious old stick. It was a shame she hadn't found anybody. Sophie was sure she would rather not be on her own. She had tried introducing people before now but Sarah had never been happy about it. Ever since her thing with that bastard Michael. She had thought about it all day, on and off, even discussing it briefly with her lunch partner who declared Sarah was a typical victim. Sophie wasn't sure she agreed with that. She had to drive frantically across town to make her three o'clock. After that she just managed to get back and stick something in the oven for later before Sarah was due to arrive. There wasn't a mark on his precious car either.

Seven times the size of Sarah's apartment, the house was situated in a nice part of town. Sarah had been only once before for Sophie's wedding back in August but found it easily enough. Sophie took her straight in to see the kittens who were feeding. Their mother, a grey tabby with white paws, lay back purring content-edly while the little bodies clambered about to get the best positions. There were four grey kittens and one white with a grey tabby marked back. Sarah fell in love with them all instantly.

'Look at him!' said Sarah laughing.

One lost his grip and in his panic dislodged all the others as he forced his way back in. Sophie let slip they were unlikely to live very long unless owners were found. Sarah kept quiet. They weren't supposed to have animals where she lived although she knew a number of people overlooked that rule. Once feeding was over, the more adventurous male of the litter settled on her lap and melted some of her reserve. Having left her clips at work her hair kept falling down and getting in the way while she played with him.

'I must get this cut!' she said, not really meaning it.

'Yes, you should,' agreed her friend, 'Nobody has long hair these days. It would do you good as well, a change of image!'

Sophie used to have her honey blonde hair long but since being married had gone for a much shorter style. It suited her and she claimed she just didn't have the time to waste. If Sarah wanted Sophie's own stylist would do a brilliant job, he was a genius with scissors. Sarah admitted there might be advantages in having short hair but she'd always worn it long. The kittens were a lot of fun and she began thinking it might be nice to have one for company. In the end, under Sophie's pressure, she agreed to take one. She could always phone later and cancel if she thought better of it. Sophie assured her she would love a cat and the company would be good for her.

'Cats have a beneficial effect on a person you know, they reduce heart rate and blood pressure and help get rid of stress.'

'Yeah, I heard that.'

'So there you are! They've got jabs and checks on Friday but the vet said they'd be ready in six weeks which will be next Sunday. You can have one any time after that really.'

It was all cut and dried to Sophie who liked arranging other people's lives. She was glad to have one less to get rid of, she couldn't keep them, Gordon wouldn't let her and she didn't want to have them put down. Gordon had only tolerated the cat, who was a stray, because Sophie had seen she was pregnant and flatly refused to turf her out.

'Did you get anything for Gordon this morning?' Sarah asked.

'Oh yes I managed to get a copy of a book by one of his favourite authors. I spent hours in that shop, the man opened up just after you left. It's like another world in there, all gloomy and quiet and everybody whispering and oh my goodness, so many books. It's like time stands still and when you get out the morning has evaporated. I only just made my lunch date.'

Leaving the kittens, they moved into the kitchen to eat.

'Here, open this!'

Sophie gave her a bottle of wine. She poured out two glasses and took them to the table while Sophie dished up. The evening passed quickly with Sophie telling her about all the things that had happened and places they'd been since the wedding. There were moments when they could still talk aimlessly and be close and after a couple of glasses of wine they were giggling like old times.

She was just getting ready to go when Gordon arrived. Sophie, fussing around him, enquired about his day but before he had time to answer began telling him about hers.

51

'Look who I met in town! She came straight over from work *and* she's going to have one of the kittens!'

'Great!' He was a bit wet from his short walk up the drive, 'Do you know it's absolutely pouring outside? How are you getting home?'

'Subway,' answered Sarah.

'You'll get soaked!'

'Perhaps I'll get a cab then.'

'No, I won't hear of it, I'll take you,' Gordon assured her.

'Don't be silly, you've only just got home, I'll be all right,' Sarah protested.

'I would,' declared Sophie, 'But I've had some wine.' She was feeling a bit sleepy anyway and was looking forward to an early night.

'That's settled then,' said Gordon and asked Sophie for his car keys.

Sarah didn't argue further and when Sophie finally retrieved the keys from the fridge, they set off. Gordon drove the big luxury car quickly through the wet streets to her not so select neighbourhood. He told her how he loved driving at night, especially in the rain.

'The family always went skiing at this time of year. We'd set off on a Saturday morning and come back after the holiday on the following Sunday night. It was exciting going out but it was the ride home I loved the best. If it was raining or snowing it made the car seem more isolated and the four of us closer. The radio would be on quiet and Mother and Father would be listening and talking in the front and my sister would have one window and I had the other and we were glued to these until we fell asleep.'

The image of somebody else's happy childhood so different from her own made Sarah feel a bit wistful. At the same time she could imagine the scene so powerfully she settled herself into the comfortable picture as they sped across town. Then Gordon started talking about his day at the bank and the warm cosiness she'd wrapped around herself was soon undone. She made as many agreeable noises as she felt were suitable while trying not to give away the fact she didn't have a clue what he was talking about.

At home there was a message on her machine for her to call Sam and Judy. The parents of an ex boy-friend, they were a warm, quiet couple she loved dearly and still sent Christmas cards to. When Sam informed her Michael had died the night before it was a complete shock. He was only a boy. Well, the same age as her.

'No,' she cried, 'He can't have!'

'I'm afraid it's true,' said Sam.

They had met at college and were so exactly opposite that at first she hadn't considered his advances as serious. He was a loud and scruffy, pale-skinned, curly-haired blond while she was quiet, dark and neat. It was a mystery why he persisted with his overtures to her. She had mistakenly believed his perseverance indicated stability.

He had a flair for photography but lacking discipline got frustrated and moody. He had a wild side and sometimes drank excessively. Initially she put his moods and occasional violent outbursts down to alcohol. It took a long time before she realised the full extent of what he was doing. His rebellious attitude had veered him into the drug culture, a world Sarah was completely innocent of and naturally avoided. When it struck her she reasoned, pleaded and did all she could to keep him straight. It was only after a desperate night when she ended up with bruises and a gashed cheek did she eventually leave him. He had never wanted to help himself and deal with his problems. It had cost her dear at the time and she went cold at the thought of him gone.

'What did he die of?' she asked the weary voice at the other end of the line.

She wished she had something adequate to say to comfort this man and his wife who had been dealt a very poor hand.

'It was AIDS.'

'But he wasn't . . .' she stammered as a void gaped inside her.

'No, apparently they reckon he must have shared a needle or something.'

'I'm sorry!' There was a long pause while he collected himself. 'How's Judy?' she asked.

'She's very good considering the circumstances. Obviously it has been hard but we're taking each day as it comes.'

'Give her my love!'

She felt for Sam and Judy who were the sweetest couple. They had always been a bit perplexed they should have brought such a noisy firework of a person into the world. Sam said they were sending over some photos of Michael's they were sure he would have wanted her to have. For their sakes she was disappointed she couldn't make the funeral. She would send flowers. When she put the phone down in her silent apartment she felt very unsubstantial. All the corners were overrun with nesting shadows yet when she turned on the central lights the stark emptiness was resounding. Dismissing the certain bleakness, she flicked off the bright lights and took her chances with the company of apprehensions. Switching the TV on, she caught the closing credits of her favourite programme. She left the TV guttering into the empty room while she showered and prepared for the morning, only snuffing it out just before she went to bed. She slept like a forest.

The journey to work next day was not so frantic as Tuesday's had been and she made sure she wore a hat. Still dark above the street lights when she set off, it was a windy day and raining buckets. The winter looked like lasting forever and she was fed up that she hardly ever saw the light of day. Just for a brief dash at lunchtime could she witness the outside world in natural colour. She yearned for the longer days of summer and being able to wear light clothes, take her lunch outside and go walking in the parks in the evening. She was yearning an eternity away. The train was more crowded this morning and there were no seats available. A short man was shoved in front of her and the adverts became the focal point. It always puzzled her why spray can enthusiasts were so determined to prove how uninteresting they were. It made her think of Michael because before he gave up trying he had always said one should be able to make an interesting photo of the most boring of subjects.

By the time she got to work her expensive Italian boots were soaked through and her feet were cold. It was a job for the fan heater and once she sat down there would be ages spent adjusting the aim of the thing. If only life were simple. Another of the girls had already opened up so she got straight on and made the coffee. Anybody else could just as easily make it but nobody did. They knew she needed it and relied on her. She wanted to tell somebody her ex-boyfriend had died but had never been in the habit of discussing her private life. She was sipping her coffee at her desk when Mr Bashford entered and marched straight to his office without saying a thing, the little eyes behind his thick glasses ignoring them all. Sarah wondered who suffered the most, Mr or Mrs. The girls exchanged glances. More generous people might stretch a sympathetic heart around the pompous figure and warm to his foibles but these girls, bruised by his prickly nature, surreptitiously gave the comical all the airing they could. He was like one of those old fashioned roses, thick with barbs. Giving him five minutes Sarah got up to take his coffee in. Dee, the early bird, appeared and volunteered herself for the job.

'I'll go, I've got to have some time off next week, my little brother is getting married. Why he has to get married in the middle of winter I don't know but then it's not so cold where he is. I hope it won't be like this anyway. Do you think Mr Bashford will mind me asking this late?'

'I shouldn't think so.'

Sarah tried to be reassuring but nobody could tell. The signs so far this morning weren't promising. As it turned out, Mr Bashford was pleased to demonstrate the generous side of his character. He could be nice. It was just her. Of course she was upset about the money, he was too. However it wasn't the end of the world. They were still very comfortable. The company was doing very nicely. She was such a greedy and selfish ... he was too exasperated to even think about it. He found some magazines to take his mind off it all and stayed out of the way reading them. The hours rattled round the clock as the office ticked over normally, everybody rushing round making lots of noise. At the end of it Sarah was so tired on the subway she kept dozing off.

When she got home and took off her boots she found they had a white mark all the way round where they'd been wet. She would have to clean them later. The large envelope Sam sent needed to be looked at first. Even as she opened the packaging the past flooded back. Seeing the photos was like having a dredger gouging up memories that had lain like happy silt at the bottom of a pond for centuries. With the jumbled up images floating before her mind's eye came the associated feelings which she could have done without. Belonging to somebody from history, she would have been happy to send them back for they were very intense and a real jolt. What was hard to take was this historical figure looked exactly like she did now, apart from the scar. In nearly ten years she hadn't changed a bit. It was as if she hadn't moved on at all. It didn't seem right. She sat for a long time with them spread out on the table trying to sort them into chronological order. Hunger pangs late in the evening brought her back to the present and reminded her she hadn't eaten. During a quick skirmish through her cupboards a can of soup caught her eye and its contents provided some filling before she went to bed.

Next morning she was tired when she woke up. What, she wondered, had she spent all night sleeping for? Her clothes were in a disagreeable mood but she eventually got inside them. Her usual breakfast wasn't enough and so an extra banana was called into service which she unzipped as she zipped off to the city. There had been no alteration in the weather, the depression affecting everything, even work. All day she was tormented by the idea that her experience with Michael had damaged her permanently. She thought her natural emotions had withered from the effects of his poisonous actions. Now she was trapped and unable to change. She tried to be rational, she had to ask herself, 'Was she happy?' If she was it didn't matter if she changed or not but the answer wouldn't come. She believed she was but actually asking something like that only made her feel miserable. In one angry thought she hated Michael, he'd done it to her, he'd ruined her life. Then reason said it wasn't fair to blame him, it was just how things happened. Her life wasn't a ruin, everybody had to make the best of things. She had a decent job, lived in a nice apartment. Her social life could have done with improving though. She never went out, she had no friends or very few anyway and those she had she was losing touch with. Her life wasn't exactly boiling over with romantic interest. In her quieter moments she sometimes constructed an idle romance around one of the residents in her block. That showed how sad she was. Maybe what her mother was always going on about, that she should make more effort, was true. She was obviously getting set in her ways. Perhaps what Sophie had said about her image was right. If that was the case then change it would be. Everywhere. That kitten would be one thing. Her hair would be another. She would get a new image. She could see herself already holding court to millions. She ended up staying late rewriting all her letters and correcting a whole mass of errors she found she had made. She wasn't normally so careless.

That evening she was watching *Millionaire*. Some quiz programmes were enjoyable. The occasional film was worthwhile but most of the time the TV was background company while she kept the place clean. Any free time in the evening she generally spent reading. There was a large bookcase at one end of her living room full of the books she'd read. Busy ironing as she watched, she had the volume up so she could hear above the hissing and sighing of the iron. The agreeable gurgling noise her iron made was the best thing about ironing only it made watching TV hard on the neighbours. She was stood, in suspense, holding the iron up in the air in its own little cloud, while a contestant pondered a question that was so easy for her. The phone rang and she grabbed it with her free hand. It was her mother, they were both watching the same thing.

'I know the answer! He was Spanish! I thought everybody knew that!'

'Why don't you go on it? You ought to go on it. You'd meet all sorts of nice people!'

In her mother's vocabulary nice meant eligible and people meant men.

'But if I went I would get questions about sport or things I just don't know about.'

They were silent while the gentleman decided Picasso was American.

'Are you coming on Sunday?' her mother asked.

'Yeah.'

'Can you get me some Glucosamine and bring it when you come?'

'Sure, is your arthritis bad?'

'This damp weather makes it worse!'

'The weather's awful isn't it? It was horrible at lunchtime when I went out, it was really windy, I nearly lost my hat.'

'Well I'm sure this stuff helps.'

'Great!'

'You know the one I have?'

'Yeah.'

'And get me a large one!'

'Okay!' She was just about to hang up when she suddenly remembered. 'I'm getting a kitten!' she said and explained the situation.

'You always wanted a kitten when you were little.'

'Did I? I can't remember!'

'Your father wouldn't let you have one.'

'Why not?'

'I don't know, he was funny about some things. When he went I was going to get you one but you didn't want one then.'

She could believe that, she'd always had an independent streak.

Friday was bright. It made an incredible difference as it was really light when she came out of the building in the morning. It was still windy and cold and she was glad of her black, tea cosy hat. She never liked the smell of the subway and sometimes it was worse than others. It wasn't often she got a seat. Today there were two seats vacant and she grabbed one and a very bulky black woman sat in the other. This lady occupied her own seat and overflowed into Sarah's. Sarah composed herself as best she could while contracting into the remaining half. At the next station the man on the other side of her left and was replaced by another huge body, a man who Sarah was certain was drunk and who smelt strongly of alcohol and sour sweat. He squashed himself into the seat and his body overflowed too. She spent the rest of the journey sitting on the edge of her seat, breathing through her mouth and wishing she had stayed standing up. Dee and the others thought it was hilarious.

'I thought you were looking a bit thinner this

morning, I wondered if you were on a diet,' Dee teased her.

'She couldn't be any thinner, even if she did go on a diet!' exclaimed Anna, a short and tubby type who was constantly waging war on her calories.

It was a very busy day. A customer was buying a whole sequence of one artist's work and she had to spend half the day at the warehouse sorting it out. The journey to the warehouse provided an enjoyable escape from routine as well as different sights. It was also convenient as she had a chance to pop into the health shop and get her mother's pills. She spent longer than she should in there looking at all the stuff they had. The only supplements she took were cod liver oil to help her migraines so she bought a pack of that. There were also some nice looking snack bars that somehow found their way into her purchases, just for her to try, as an experiment. They did brighten up the afternoon shift, so it wasn't a bad experiment.

That evening she collected up Michael's photos in their proper order, packed them into a box and stored them away. It was hardly worth buying an album for them as she was unlikely to show anybody. It was sad really. Too tired to think she sat watching a mindless love triangle go round and round and finally go pear shaped on the TV. Eventually giving up the delights of relentless trivia, she clicked the remote and prised herself out of her settee. She had a shower before turning in.

Next day it was up for work as usual. Saturdays were covered on a rota and this week was her turn. She didn't mind too much as she had the previous Monday off. They opened an hour later than on weekdays which just gave her time to get to the pet shop and buy the things she would need for the kitten. The pet store owner was very helpful and thorough and explained everything in a deep, deep voice she could hardly believe was real. He was even thinner than her and having ginger hair was a mixture of beanpole and carrot. Sarah couldn't help wondering how he survived the urban environment. If he would regard the natural environment with warmth or suspicion, surely his obvious sympathy with animals suggested a leaning . . . she had to quickly derail this train of thought before the comical image became too much. He was too nice a man to have comical images about. Amazed at how much stuff was needed, she had a job carrying it. She dumped it all back at her apartment and set off again. It was another bright but cold day. Typically it was always pleasant on the Saturdays she was down to work. The subway was nice and empty and there was room to spread out. A bit different from her journey the day before, she reflected. It must have looked really silly, her, slender as she was, stuck between two huge bodies like that. It would surely have made an amusing photo. Again poor Michael was occupying her thoughts. It was to be his cremation on Monday. At the other end she thought it would be worth getting off one stop early and walking the extra, take advantage of the dry day to get some exercise. She needed to walk briskly to keep warm in the shadows of the big buildings. After opening up and putting the coffee on she was ready to face the day. The gallery could be busy as there were sometimes a lot of customers to deal with which meant the time went quickly. She stopped off on the way home to get a take-away meal. After eating that she left the radio on in the kitchen and curled up on the settee with a mug of hot chocolate and her book.

Sunday she was up fairly early. Every four weeks she made the journey across town to see her mother and they went together to church. It was a dry and bright day but bitterly cold and they didn't stop afterwards to chat with their friends as usual. They were glad to get back inside her mother's small apartment. Although getting on in years and beginning to shrink, her mother was still mobile and healthy and was as vocal as ever. Sarah expected an earful when she mentioned cutting her hair. Always having had it long it was a drastic step for her and she needed support rather than the tirade she got.

'What do you want to cut your lovely hair for? You're starting to get sloppy, keep on and you'll lose your self-respect altogether and you'll end up not caring how you look at all.'

She had a habit of answering her own questions which was somehow worse than letting Sarah answer them for herself.

'You're making a mistake, men prefer long hair! When are you going to get a man? You'll never get one at this rate!'

Inevitably Sarah had given her even more cause for concern and once she got started it was best to keep quiet.

'I don't know why you don't get out more, meet more people. You need to use your charms.'

'Mother!'

'You got charms! You oughta learn to use them properly. Not on those half hopes you call artists.'

She could never resist a dig at Sarah's past failure.

'You know Michael died on Monday?'

This gave her mother some pause for thought but not much.

'What did he die of?'

'I don't know, drugs I suppose.'

There was no point in being specific.

'I always knew he would end up in an early grave. I don't know what you saw in him in the first place.'

'He could be very sweet!'

She wasn't allowed to expand on his good points before the career advice returned.

'You want to give up that job with Bash and Howells. You're not getting anywhere, the firm's too small, you can't get promotion. You've been doing the same thing for five years now, it's time you moved on. Why don't you apply for that other company? You could really get on in a bigger organisation. I suppose you've got no ambition. Oh well, I did my best!'

Mary was more and more concerned about Sarah. She didn't seem to ever go out. Her friend's children were out all the time or if not they had families of their own. No matter what she said she couldn't get it into Sarah's head that life whizzed by only too quickly. If she didn't do something it would be gone before she knew it. She knew Sarah had had a bad time with Michael and she felt awkward because she had opposed it, not liking him from the beginning. The trouble was that if she said anything, which of course she did, all the time, it only made matters worse. She felt completely powerless. She knew the scar had affected her and she was reluctant to be always pushing. But then she didn't understand her daughter because half of the time she was really brassy about the scar and then the other half she would just retreat right back into her shell.

'Don't be silly, of course I want to get on, it's just . . .'
Her mother wasn't listening.

'Go where the money is, that's your best bet, join the Teller Corporation!' she suggested, coming out of her reverie.

This was a huge conglomerate which had a subsidiary company working in the same field so Mary felt it would be a good career move. Teller, the man behind the corporation, happened to be one of the richest people in the city and a sponsor of the arts, a very prominent figure. There was something in the family for his brother was a world-renowned concert pianist and composer. Both had got to the top in their own field. The head of the Teller corporation, William, had been fascinated from an early age by the money markets. From small beginnings he had built a fortune. He now ran an empire that had interests in electronics, chemicals, plastics and speciality food products as well as art.

As she made her way back home, the low afternoon sunlight was setting the tops of glass buildings on fire, Sarah considered her mother's exhortations. In some ways she didn't want to leave Bash and Howells. Staff kept changing all the time, she had been there as long as anybody, knew all the ropes and it was nice to be senior. Neither of the founders was very pleasant but they left her alone to get on with things which she did and she enjoyed that. They paid her quite well too which was another thing. She didn't fancy the idea of starting fresh and new in a place and having to get used to new routines. Then again perhaps she was getting stuck. Of course her mother was right that she couldn't go further but what could she do? You can't just walk into another company and demand to be employed. You couldn't guarantee success somewhere else either. Nothing was ever simple. She would have to keep an eye open for jobs in the papers.

The alarm on Monday morning put Sarah in a slapping mood. After slapping a flannel about her person she slapped on some make-up. Jumping into her usual black clothes, she gulped down some breakfast. Woe betide anybody who got in her way, if they did she would give them a slap. She was going to change, everything was going to change or she would know the reason why. By the end of the day she would be a different person. As she slapped the elevator button the phrase 'slap-happy' pinged into her mind and she smiled to herself going down. Even colder than the day before, it was another bright morning. It was a big day for her as her hair was coming off. It had always been her pride and joy but lately, what with one thing and another, it had been annoying her. As usual she endured the raucous subway squash, buffeting and jostle through half-open eyes, only opening them fully when she reached the comparative calm and safety of her workplace. Once there, on went the coffee maker and in came the girls. Another week began.

While she was rummaging around in the foyer cupboards during the morning Mr Teller turned up. A very good-looking and distinctive man, he wore the tanned skin of the wealthy outdoors. He was far older than her but handsomely rich and known to be very charitable. He asked to see Mr Bashford and her heart rattled about in her chest like anything when she showed him the way. There was a lot of office interest in this event and a number of the girls discussed, quite shamelessly, the lengths they might be prepared to go to in trapping a Mr Teller and his money.

'Wouldn't you do anything for a man with eyes like his?' Dee enquired. 'I could look into them forever!'

'He's married!' said Anna, shocked.

'Who's worried about that?' the others giggled.

When Teller left he thanked Sarah.

'You're in there!' the others yelled even before the door had closed.

Later on, at lunchtime, she shook and brushed her long hair for the last time and set off for the salon. There was a quantity of black, plastic bin bags piled high, smelling high, on the sidewalk outside the hairdressers. Inside one of the hairdressers was telling a client that, 'They', should have been the day before to clear it up.

'I've just been on to them now and *the same man* who said it would be done today said it would be done tomorrow. This city is going downhill fast!' she heard the distracted man exclaim.

The receptionist asked her name and then took her through to Dominic, 'The genius with the scissors'. Dominic's warm, chatty nature put her at ease straight away. He was very sympathetic and played up the benefits of short hair.

As he began cutting he asked, 'How did you get your scar?'

'What scar?' she demanded icily, staring hard at him in the mirror.

Dominic was quiet for a minute but was too bubbly a person to shut up for long and Sarah was happy he quickly found better subjects for conversation and forgave him his indiscretion. He styled her hair carefully and she was happy to accept his advice. It was quite a relaxing business and she had to make an effort to keep her eyes open. When it was done Sarah couldn't believe the transformation, her face looked so different. She tottered back to the office in a sort of daze. All afternoon she couldn't stop trying to push back the hair she'd just lost and kept starting at the draught on her neck. The other girls all said how nice it looked but she wasn't sure if she trusted them.

After work she made her way to Sophie's, this time to pick up the kitten who was now old enough to leave his mother. It meant more subway. When she got there Sophie admired her new hairstyle and was obviously pleased, perhaps too smug Sarah thought. She stayed non-committal although she was glad for some approval. She would have to make her own way home as Gordon had taken his car and Sophie was still without hers.

'I should have got a hire car really but I thought it would only be a few days and it wasn't worth the bother,' she explained. 'By the way,' she continued, 'Did you see the papers yesterday?'

'No.'

'You remember Gordon taking you home last week?'

'Yes.'

'He said he was telling you about the Bashford seniors.'

'Oh, was he? I don't remember.'

'No he said he didn't think you cottoned on.'

'Oh what about them?'

'Well you know how wealthy they are? Well apparently they've cut their family off completely and have set up a trust fund to look after Third World children. Gordon was working on setting it all up. Of course he couldn't say anything directly but now it's been in the papers.'

'Oh!' exclaimed Sarah, 'That's why Mr Bashford has been in such a bad mood lately! Each morning he comes in with a ferocious scowl on his face and just hides in his office all day. That explains it.'

They continued chatting for a while but Sarah didn't want to stay too late and she wouldn't even stop for something to eat. Sarah felt so cruel when she pushed the kitten's unwilling body into the little box Sophie gave her for him to travel in, his plaintive mewing tugging at her heartstrings. Almost as soon as she got outside the heavens opened. It was as if they thought she was cruel too. To keep the rain off she had to hold the box under her coat, which was very awkward. The poor little kitten was very good, he sat quiet all the way, wide-eyed and probably terrified. When she got back she cooked herself a quick meal and then spent what was left of the evening playing with her new companion, taking his photo and showing him the apartment, his new home. He was a little, mottled grey fellow with green eyes and an inquisitive outlook. She named him James.

That night was filled with a horrible dream. She had lost something and was running through an endless version of her childhood home and in each room couldn't find what was supposed to be there. She sat up clutching the duvet. Her neck was cold and she felt empty. James was sleeping soundly. Checking the clock, there was an hour to go before the alarm so she wrapped the duvet around herself, turned over and went back to sleep. She felt fine when the alarm went and sat for a while trying to remember what had happened before it all came back, engulfing her like an avalanche. Chewing her way through breakfast, she tried analysing it. If it had been about her hair it was weird to feel so desperate. It would grow back in a few months if she really wanted it long. There was no reason to be so anxious.

James seemed to be looking for his brothers and sisters and trotted all through the apartment making little noises. She hated leaving him on his own all day and couldn't bear to think of him being lonely. She put plenty of water and a little food down. As she cleaned her teeth and studied her reflection in the bathroom mirror she decided Dominic had done well for her. Outside it was overcast and damp. She was glad it was a bit milder and getting lighter in the mornings. Fighting through the rush hour commuters was the same. Although she knew it was daft, she took some polaroids of James into the office to put on her desk. They were noticed straightaway and she ended up having long discussions with the other girls about each of their various pets. Unfortunately Monday's extra travelling and excitement had taken its toll and by the end of the day tiredness had set in. On the way home the vision of ready food in the delicatessen enticed her in there and soon filled a couple of bags to save her cooking. Half-expecting to find the kitten had demolished her apartment, she was getting more apprehensive the nearer home she got. As she stood waiting for the elevator another person arrived. Flicking a casual glance at the newcomer, her heart began beating fast.

'Why Mr Teller!' she exclaimed. He jumped, not recognising her.

'I beg your pardon, do I know you?'

'We met briefly yesterday, I work at Bash and Howells.'

'Oh yes, I was there yesterday but the girl I spoke to had long hair, that wasn't you!'

'Yes, it was. I had it cut during lunch yesterday, it's easier to manage being shorter!'

'I'm sorry I didn't recognise you for a minute.'

'Of course you wouldn't.'

There was a pause while the elevator arrived and they entered. She said the first thing that came into her head.

'I'm hoping to find my apartment in one piece.' Teller raised his eyebrows, his clear blue eyes studying her intently.

'Shouldn't it be?'

'It should be but I've got a new kitten, I only brought him home yesterday and I had to leave him alone all day today. I'm just hoping he hasn't wrecked the place.'

'I'm sure he's been all right. I expect he's been asleep all day, that's what cats usually do! We have a cat at home and he sleeps all day and I'm sure he sleeps all night as well. Mind you he's getting a bit elderly now.' Sarah was grateful for his kindness but didn't pursue any further conversation save to say, 'This is me!' and 'Bye!' when she stepped out of the elevator. At home she was greeted by a pathetic grey bundle who hadn't destroyed the apartment at all. Gathering him in her arms, she tried to make up for being away so long. All the while she played with James she couldn't stop wondering what Mr Teller was doing in the building. It was strange, a man like him, here.

Wednesday was a busy and difficult day. It started badly as it was pouring heavily and by the time she got to work her boots were soaked. Again she had cold feet. Again she had to battle with the fan heater. Mr Howells, the junior partner and driving force of the business was due in as well. Tall and thin like a crane, he had a stoop and manner of a vulture. His idea of social grace was what other people said before eating. Lank hair and travel-stained clothes belied his wealth. Most of his life was spent either on a jet or on the way to or from one as he trawled the world looking for new or interesting items. When he arrived the office was always turned upside down. He soon had his secretaries rushing around organising his travel arrangements and most of his personal life. When he went they all heaved a sigh of relief, thankful he had gone.

This morning he and Bashford had an almighty argument before they each stormed out of the office. As this was a lot longer row and more noisy than usual, everybody was uncertain what was going on and Sarah tried her best to keep everything running smoothly. There was a lot of new stuff coming in which she had to check as well as keep up with her normal tasks. It was still raining in her lunch hour which she spent trying to find a present for Sophie. She ended up with wet boots again and a set of fridge magnets which were so sweet she was tempted to keep them herself and look for something else for Sophie on another day. Back in the office the atmosphere made the afternoon drag on and she was relieved when it was finally over and she could start the journey home.

She reached her building at the same time as the man she'd noticed before. This man intrigued her. He wasn't bad looking in a dark, angular sort of way. Today he was wet, trickles of water running from his hair down his face. Of average height and clean shaven, he was quick and purposeful. He often carried parcels and bags with obviously peculiar shaped things in them that she couldn't help but notice. Plainly he was some sort of collector but what it was he collected she had no idea. He was carrying a large, wet box which made getting in the elevator difficult. As change was still on the agenda she racked her brain for an opening that wasn't pathetic or corny and hit on one that was both.

'It's a big box!'

'Yes,' the man answered abruptly as if to forestall further conversation.

Sarah accordingly remained silent and considered how unhelpful brains actually were. Why hadn't she stuck with the weather? Nobody minds talking about the weather. As she entered her apartment she looked for her pet. The night before he had met her, calling pathetically. Today, while she was out, a more confident James had investigated the apartment fully. Certain there was more to the world than he'd found so far he needed to check it out. When Sarah provided a gap he was off. Seeing he was not inside she looked back into the hall and saw his tail disappearing into the elevator.

'Oh hell!' Dropping her bags she ran back down the hall, 'Hey!'

Too late, the elevator was gone. She dashed up the stairs and got to the next level just as the box man was going into his apartment. He was 609, the apartment directly above hers.

'Excuse me, oh, sorry,' she was puffed. 'Excuse me but did you notice my kitten? He slipped into the elevator with you.'

'No I didn't, mind you I can't see much with this.'

'I wonder if you could check if he's in your apartment, he might have gone in as you opened the door.'

'I'll have a look, hold on!' he said, closing the door.

Sarah nipped back and jabbed the button for the elevator which hadn't moved and the door opened to reveal an empty cubicle. Whispering to herself, 'Please, please!' she waited by the door. In a moment it reopened and the box man appeared holding the escapee.

'Here, I have to hand it to him he has a fair turn of speed when he wants to use it, luckily I caught him before he got under the furniture!'

'Oh thanks, thank you very much!'

'He's a cute little chap!'

'Yes, I only got him on Monday. I hope he won't keep escaping.'

'You'll need to be quick to stop him!' He held the kitten up in the air, 'He looks like a tiny raincloud!'

Sarah wished she'd been the one to make that observation.

'He can get a bit damp,' she said.

'Can't we all?' he looked down at his wet raincoat that was dripping onto the floor.

'That's for sure, hasn't it been awful today? My boots are ruined, it was the same last Wednesday!'

She showed her boots with their white marks.

'That's too bad.' He handed her the kitten and asked, 'What do you call him?'

'"James."'

'Like the English Chauffeur,' he put on an upper class English accent and said, 'James go outside and butter the rolls!'

Sarah smiled and said, 'I just like the name. Do you have a cat yourself?' she asked.

'No, the family did when I was young.'

'Would you have one now?' It would be nice to find a home that might take another one of Sophie's kittens.

'I'd love one but I'm out a lot of the day, it wouldn't be fair.'

'What do you do?'

'I drive a bus. You're full of questions aren't you!'

'Oh, oh, I'm sorry. I didn't mean . . .' Although she was she didn't want to appear nosy so she turned to go. 'I'd better let you get on, thank you for finding my kitten! Bye!'

'Bye!'

Thursday was overcast. On the subway it struck her how Sophie had used the phrase, 'Nobody has long hair these days'. There were lots of women with long hair in the carriage she was sat in. When Sophie spoke it was her circle that was all that mattered. And it was this attitude, as much as anything, that was letting them drift apart. It wasn't that their worlds were different, she could deal with that. It was that Sophie wasn't the slightest bit interested in hers. It was always her that made the effort for Sophie and the stupid thing was Sophie was better situated, was wealthier, didn't work and owned a car. It would be so much easier for her. She guessed her own poor orbit was just not interesting enough for Sophie to be bothered with.

At work the founders didn't come in all day and could not be reached. They weren't at the warehouse, nobody knew where they were. Sarah was cross that they had not said anything to anybody. It wasn't fair. Apart from that it was a fairly typical day which she spent reading the mail, checking stock and writing the outgoing mail while everybody else rushed round waving bits of paper.

Like a surgical excision, finding out what he did had removed nearly all of her curiosity about the bus driver. She saw him again when she came home on Thursday evening, he was going out while she was coming in and she acknowledged him without any real interest. This time he was more talkative.

'I was thinking about yesterday, I didn't mean to sound impatient, it had just been a long day.'

'No, it doesn't matter. You were right anyway, I shouldn't be nosy, I've always been the same.'

'You can't be alive if you're not curious.'

'That's true,' she agreed and made as to move on.

He continued talking with, 'So what do you do?'

She couldn't help putting on a bit of a voice to say she worked for Bash and Howells. It was a small firm and few people outside the art world had ever heard of it but sometimes saying the name as if everybody knew it shut people up.

'Oh,' he said, she felt there was a certain coolness in his voice. 'Which shop do you work at?'

'Oh no, there's only one gallery, we're not far from the city centre! Have you heard of Bash and Howells?' she asked, not believing he could have.

'Yes, I have as it happens!' How? she wondered.

'Oh, it's quite a specialist company!'

'You like it there?'

'I do actually, I'm kept very busy but it's interesting. How do you know about them?'

She was curious again now.

'Oh, somebody I knew had dealings with Nicholas Howells,' he gave one of the founders' names, so he did know and wasn't just saying. Very intriguing.

'It was a while back now,' he said dismissively.

'Oh!'

Her surprise at his knowledge of her firm and his apparent dislike of it left her at a loss for something to say.

'Anyhow I'd better be going!' He paused, 'It's funny I always liked your hair long but I have to say this new style looks good although it's quite different. Anyway, see you later!'

He turned and left. It was true, he had noticed her before and had wanted to talk to her. She was a very

76

attractive girl and always looked smart. He had found before now that he was generally on a different wavelength from other people so he had made no attempt at introduction. He'd given all that up a long time ago. The expression, 'Marching to a different drum,' best described him and apart from his job he lived a solitary life. He was very lucky in some ways as he knew what he wanted to do and did it. In other ways he was disappointed and frustrated. He would rather not have been sexually inactive but was philosophical about it conceding that he could at least pursue his interests undistracted. He had met several outwardly attractive but superficial and scheming women and was glad to be free of such destructive entanglements. It could take a long time finding out about a person's true nature and he didn't really have enough time as it was. This rationalism, however, didn't get rid of his natural desire for female company and at odd moments like this it overtook his distance. As he turned away he wished vehemently he hadn't volunteered the compliment, wished he hadn't spoken at all. Why couldn't he just be silent?

'Th . . . thank you,' Sarah faltered, flattered.

At the same time, however, she was wondering about his dislike of her firm. Not that it mattered but what did he have against Howells? He wasn't at all popular but she wanted to know exact details. Then again he said he liked her hair, he said he liked it! Not only that he said he *always* liked her hair long so he must have noticed her before. When? She drifted up to her apartment and this time she was ready to scoop up James if he came out but he didn't. Once inside she picked him up, took him into the kitchen and fed him his tea before having her own.

Later on that night there was a knock on her door.

Outside was a lady speaking a torrent of Spanish to an eager-faced little boy whose expression dropped when he saw Sarah.

'Yes?'

'Oh please, Señor Brandon, is he in?'

'I beg your pardon?'

'Are we on the wrong floor?'

'Who do you want?'

'Señor Brandon, the coach driver.'

'What's he done?'

'He saved my boy's life. He saved my grandson from a terrible accident.'

'What, today?' she demanded, naturally concerned.

'Oh no, not today, over four years now.'

'Oh,' she relaxed again, he was nothing to her after all. 'Well I know there's a coach driver upstairs, he lives directly above. I should think he's the man you're after.'

'We do have the wrong floor, sorry, so sorry to disturb you.'

'No trouble!'

She closed the door and found she was reopening the case of Busman or Brandon, if that was his name. 'Fancy that!' she thought. The hero type didn't really appeal to her, not that there was anything against them. Then again he didn't strike one as the hero type anyway. His joke suddenly clicked. 'Butter the Rolls,' it was quite clever. It hadn't made any sense to her at the time. James needed attention so she had to put these thoughts aside. They had a brilliant game of chase the string round every room and the evening vanished.

Sarah didn't get a full night's sleep that night. At about four o'clock in the morning James decided to work off an excess of energy he'd built up by tearing round the apartment and straight across her bed as fast as he could. The shock of several, 'Tours' ousted her from her dreams completely and she got up and made herself a hot milk drink. An hour later, once she was wide awake, James lay fast asleep on her bed as she absent-mindedly stroked him and worried about her job.

The alarm dragged her from a very comfortable place straight into a world moving twice as fast as she was. Not being able to function properly didn't help and neither did any of the clocks. Swallowing her breakfast whole she dashed out to hit the wet, early morning rush. The wind tugged at her coat and scarf. It was the usual degrading squash in the subway, the squabbling train and pressing crowds. Again Mr Bashford and Mr Howells were absent from the office and there were phone calls all day from newspapers. Being completely in the dark about what was going on she wasn't too pleased. She didn't know how many times she explained that she couldn't help and the founders were unavailable. There was no shortage of theories among the girls to explain this absence. Some of them were very amusing if a bit crude and they managed at least to have a good laugh at the expense of the bosses. It was also the day of Dee's brother's wedding and she wondered how it would go. It certainly wasn't wedding weather here but she hoped they were more lucky. She had mixed feelings about weddings. They were nice occasions but she always felt a bit redundant. Even at Sophie's she hadn't felt fully involved. Nearly all her friends were married now and the prospect of her following suit was as unlikely as a world at peace. She knew Sophie had tried getting her to meet new people but she had hated the whole thing of being 'set up'. She would rather stay single than meet people that way.

At the end of what had been a long and gruelling week Sarah came home on Friday to find the police department all over the place. She didn't want to believe the horrifying news that there had been a double murder in one of the apartments. Hardly knowing anybody in the building, she hadn't known the victims. It was frightening to think the killer was still free, maybe even still there. In the hall she talked to a couple of residents she'd only ever nodded to before. They were all eager to know exactly what had happened and each was asking the next in case they had the slightest extra detail. The story going round was that an ex-lover of one of the victims had broken in late the night before and in a fit of jealousy had killed them both. Apparently there had been trouble before. The bodies had been stabbed repeatedly and there was blood everywhere in the apartment. The superintendent had found them after seeing the door was left open. They said he had needed treatment for shock. The incident happened on the floor above hers and when she asked which number was relieved to be told 611.

A pair of detectives approached her and one of them asked for her details and if she might have any information. Not having seen or heard anything, she wasn't any help. The elevators were being checked for forensic evidence so they were temporarily out of action. There was nothing for it but to climb the stairs, just what she needed after the week she'd had. On the second floor a pair of eyes were peeping out from behind a door. A wave of panic surged through her before the door opened and a small dark figure appeared. Sarah had seen this lady before but had never spoken, now everybody was talking.

'Oh you scared me!' said Sarah.

'Oh I'm sorry, my dear, I was just keeping an eye out, you can't be too careful. I'm so glad it wasn't you. I said to Jerry, my husband, 'I hope it's not that girl with the lovely hair,' but I don't know who it was yet.'

'No I don't know who it was either.'

Sarah moved her head but the weight had gone, the woman didn't seem to notice.

'What a terrible thing. You don't expect it to happen here, not in a nice building like this. What is the world coming to? It's getting so you can't sleep in your own bed at night!'

'Maureen, leave the neighbours alone!' her husband called from inside the apartment.

'That's Jerry now! It wasn't that girl with the lovely hair!' she shouted back to him. 'I was just telling her how we hoped it hadn't been her, she doesn't know who it was either.'

'Don't stand out there, if you want to talk bring her inside, let her sit down!'

'No really I have to get home.'

'She has to go home!'

James was evidently pleased to see her when she got back and she was very glad he was there. She kept him on her lap all evening and fussed him terribly. Later in the evening Sophie rang and told her she was welcome to come over and spend the night with them, she would send Gordon over if she wanted. He had been watching the news, seen the item and had remembered her address. Sarah didn't really want to go and made an excuse that she was already on her way somewhere else. As well as the chain she usually kept on she shot the bolt on her door and also pushed a chair under the handle of her bedroom door before going to bed. Realising this was unnecessary and she was overreacting she got up and put it back in its place leaving the door ajar as she normally did. There were policemen on duty both down and upstairs. 15 minutes later she crept back out of bed, shut the door and slid the chair under the handle again. Even then she lay awake for a long time starting at the slightest sound.

Despite her anxiety the night before she woke up fresh and early on Saturday morning without the alarm. Lying in was an enjoyable luxury she didn't often indulge in. The weekend was the one time of the week when she felt the apartment was her own and not just a launchpad for work and she didn't like to waste it. Armed only with a small watering can she splashed her way round her plants, giving words of encouragement to them all as she went, eventually ending up in the living room, her favourite place. It was a restful room in cream and pale blue, featuring a cream carpet and a round blue Chinese rug in front of the settee. She was proud of the decoration. Pulling open the drapes, she surveyed the world outside. It was a bright morning with plenty of blue between the white clouds crossing the sky. She remembered being a gullible six-year-old and her father telling her that clouds were huge envelopes full of air mail. He said the more letters people wrote the worse the weather got. That was why he wouldn't write because he loved the sunshine and when the sun shone it reminded him of her. He had been a true salesman. He had left them for one of his young and attractive prospects when Sarah was still in junior school. She still would have preferred something more solid than knowing he might think of her if it was fine.

The blocks nearby framed some impressive long views. From her window it was city one way and city the other but it was her city and her view and she loved it. On a clear day like this she could pick out the spires of four churches. There was always something to look at but she didn't want to spend too long. After breakfast she set off for a quick shop. With the jobs out of the way she could use the afternoon constructively. She might visit a gallery or museum or if the weather was cold she might just stay in and catch up with the latest novel. Outside it wasn't so windy and it was still fresh but definitely a bit warmer. In her kitchen when she returned and unpacked and everything was spread over the table and side it was obvious she had forgotten to buy a newspaper. She went out again to get this indispensable item. Leafing through the paper in the street on her way back she bumped into him just outside their building. He was carrying groceries this time and they stopped to talk.

'Had to get a paper, see if they say anything about, you know.

She couldn't say the terrible word.

'Is there?'

'Not so far.' As she turned the pages she realised their position and that she would prefer to be under cover. 'Let's move inside!' she suggested, 'Out of the way.'

'Out of the way?'

'You know, birds and things!' she explained as vaguely as possible as they entered the building. 'What's this? "Space debris found in City harbour!" had to happen sooner or later I suppose. Oh yes here we are, it says, "Police were called yesterday to the scene of a gruesome double murder at this apartment block, details will be released when next of kin have been informed." It isn't very much!'

'Never satisfied!'

'I know, it's awful isn't it! Morbid! It's got everybody talking though, I'd hardly spoken to anyone in the building before last night.'

'That's it! You've got it! The answer to lack of conversation, simple, get somebody to murder your neighbour!'

She noticed he had a habit of running his hand through his short, dark hair and messing it up.

'No, don't say that!'

'I can see the headlines now, 'Murder rate soars as people start talking!' It would be counter-productive in the end because there would be nobody left to talk. Oh well, try again. Did you get the two detectives asking you questions, or one of them anyway?'

'Yeah.'

'Was it just me or was the quiet one really creepy?'

'He was a bit. He couldn't have had a dirtier raincoat.'

'The one who asked all the questions was bad enough but boy he was weird! I named them Cheap and Cheerful.'

Sarah laughed at this. He had a sort of half smile which just added a small crease to the corner of his eyes and curled up the very edges of his lips.

'Cheapowski!' she corrected him.

He continued, 'Digging in the dirt seems to have affected them. They should have been scatologists. It made me think of a joke. What did the scatologist with ennui say?'

'I don't know and I'm not sure I really want to.'

84

'Wrong, he said, 'I'm just going through the motions'.'

He said it in such a morose way that despite herself she giggled before telling him how disgusting he was.

'Okay,' he said, 'Did you hear about the scatologist who died?'

'No.'

'He was interred!'

'Oh do you have to?' she said, trying not to laugh. 'Where do you get these from?'

'I just think of them.'

'I wish you wouldn't!'

'They strike me as amusing!' he declared.

Making an effort to keep her mind on the serious job of straightening and folding the newspaper she knew her face let her down.

'What was that?' he asked.

'Nothing, I was just thinking about James and his antics,' she lied. 'He fell off the back of the settee last night. He likes to sit up there and he must have fallen asleep because there was this thud and he dashed across the floor and stopped in the middle of the room and began to wash his face as if nothing had happened at all. It was really funny!'

'Cats are great!' he said.

She had to ask him, 'Is your name Brandon?'

'That's right, who told you?'

'Your visitors yesterday got the wrong floor and knocked on my door first. I live directly below you.'

'Oh!'

'She mentioned your heroism.'

'Oh.'

'So how did it happen?'

'What my heroism? Oh it's nothing!' he said very nonchalant and reaching for a bunch of celery from his bag he explained, 'I eat a stick of this kryptonite every day and . . .'

'No, the accident I mean!'

'Oh that. You really want to know?'

'Not if you don't want!'

'No, it doesn't matter, it's a long time ago now. It was just a nasty pile up and I happened to get there first. I'd seen it happen up in front of me and I'd pulled over and had my hazards on. It was terrible weather, pouring with rain. I was lucky to get the boy clear but there were some who were not so lucky. There were cars still coming too fast to stop crashing into it and then one of the cars went up. Just, boom, like that, like a fireball. I had an empty coach so they used it to keep people warm and dry till the emergency services got things sorted out. The boy wouldn't let go of me. He lost his Mum and Dad. It was a real nightmare. Not very pleasant.'

'Oh my, it sounds horrible!'

'The grandmother has almost adopted me. I'm not sure why really but she's very nice. For months they invited me round. They're a nice family, good, hard-working people, always made me feel at home. For a long time I thought I was helping them but now I think they helped me a lot more. It's funny, I felt bad for a long time without realising how bad. I saw the doctor after that and she said it was normal. I suppose it was stupid not to see the doctor straight away but it hadn't been me in the accident, I hadn't been injured. You don't think.'

'No, of course you wouldn't,' she said.

'I tried to help the boy all I could, he's a great kid. He's like a little brother to me now. It was a terrible thing to happen, nobody needs that sort of thing. After a while I thought they would forget but of course it's his birthday so she has to remember. She makes me a cake every year. Do you like cake? Do you want to come up now and have some coffee and cake? It's very nice.'

'Yeah, okay, that would be great!'

She agreed without thinking but once they were in the elevator all sorts of doubts and fears began welling up in her mind. Saying yes like that had been careless, especially after what had happened. He must have sensed she had some misgivings for he said,

'You don't have to come up, I could bring the cake to you or you can skip it altogether if you want.'

Then again she didn't know why she trusted him but she did.

'No I'm fine! I need some coffee anyway.'

As he let her into his apartment she couldn't help commenting, 'This is nice. Our apartments are the same but the decoration makes them so different. This is much nicer than mine, I love the colours. Can I see the rest?'

'You want to inspect the place? Well it's a bit of a mess in that room but you can see the others if you like.'

'Oh!' she exclaimed when she stepped into his bedroom, 'Oh!' She wasn't sure what else to say. Fixed to the wall above the bed like some sort of trophy was an enormous screw. She turned to go back out.

'You don't like my screw! It's eighteen feet long. I wanted the longest screw I could possibly have in the bedroom.'

'You definitely have a vulgar side!'

'I wouldn't say that, earthy maybe, not vulgar.'

'It's a bit overpowering.'

'Good! It amused me at the time.'

'It is long, how did you manage to get it here?'

87

'I built it myself, it's actually made in sections and fitted together. Anyway, tour over, let's have some coffee!'

He led her into the kitchen. It was very nice if a bit dated with pine everywhere. There was a large Windsor armchair and a couple of ordinary wheel back chairs around a pine table. Still it was clean. On the side was a small gold trashcan encrusted with diamonds.

Noticing it Sarah declared, 'Oh, isn't that sweet!'

'You don't think it's rubbish?' he asked, smiling.

'No, where did you get it?'

'That would be saying.'

'If those were real it would be worth millions,' she said, pointing to the diamonds.

'Something is only worth money if it's for sale and that isn't!'

Lifting it to have a better look at it Sarah exclaimed in surprise, 'Boy it's heavy!'

'Gold is heavy!'

She looked at him and laughed, enjoying his joke.

'Yeah sure, you drive a bus!'

He put the trashcan under the counter where it belonged and set about making fresh coffee.

'Actually, although I said I drive a bus it's not true anymore. They promoted me, I'm in the office now, I just sit around all day answering the phone, making sure shifts are covered, working out rotas and things like that.'

'Sounds like you're not so happy with your promotion.'

'I don't know, driving is hard, or not really hard but there's a lot of responsibility and you are concentrating all the time. Also it's tangible, I prefer dealing with tangible things. Then again it's nice not to be on shifts, some of the driver's shifts are horrible, early mornings, late nights and stuff. I don't know, I'm wondering if it isn't time to move on. I've got my holidays coming up so I'm going to have a big think about everything and get my life sorted out.'

'Oh that sounds ominous. Isn't your life sorted out already?'

'Mostly I'd say yes but things change. You set off in one direction and end up going in another. You always need to make adjustments. Everybody changes!'

'I suppose so,' she said, not believing she had.

He poured the coffee and cut her a slice of cake.

'This is delicious!' she said, munching away.

'It is nice isn't it. She's a good cook and a very generous person.'

It wasn't long before the murder entered the conversation.

'I didn't know them but then I hardly know anybody in the building. Did you know them?' she asked.

'Not really. I spoke to them once or twice. They were quite friendly. I think they were both younger than me. It's horrible knowing they've been blotted out just like that. It really makes you think.'

'It's ghastly,' she agreed.

'I've got a feeling I'm a suspect,' he confessed.

'Why?' she demanded, horrified.

'Well, I live right next door and I've got no alibi. Although I haven't admitted it, I was out when it was supposed to have happened and I wouldn't be able to prove where I was.'

'Where were you?'

'Out walking.'

'What out walking the streets at night?' She was incredulous, 'Isn't that dangerous?'

'It can be but if you're careful it's okay. I've always

been lucky and I love the feel of places at night. I think it's important to keep in touch with things as they are and not just how we want them to be.'

'Maybe you're right but I still wouldn't go out walking at night!'

They talked about her job and the firm she worked for and she asked why she felt he didn't like it.

'It's only as far as I'm concerned, people like Mr Bashford are just leeches.'

'I beg your pardon!'

She bristled. Despite his faults she was loyal toward her employer and would have said more if this bus driver had given her a chance. Sadly, the romantic character that she'd outlined for him wasn't appearing. He was less polished and was not exactly the comfortable fit she had sometimes imagined.

'He used his family's wealth to set up a trendy business. It's all geared to make him look important.'

Having disagreed with him at first, she had to concede that in fact he wasn't far off the mark. If that was what he was trying to say she might overlook his clumsy approach.

'Mr Bashford has a lot of good qualities!'

She tried to stick up for her boss.

'Of course the real dodgy business is the stuff Nicholas Howells brings back from his jaunts. I guess you probably don't see much of that.'

She was unprepared for this and didn't know what to say. When he offered to make some more coffee she realised the morning was passing and there were things she had to do. Declining his offer, she thanked him and got up to go.

As she was leaving she decided to ask him out.

'Do you fancy coming to an art exhibition preview this evening?'

'I don't know about that.'

'Please, I need an escort?'

She smiled charmingly at him.

'In that case how could I refuse?'

'After all this horror I thought it might be nice.'

'Yeah you're right, what time?'

'Say seven,'

'Okay.'

Back at her apartment the telephone was ringing. She picked it up and was almost deafened by the blast of her mother's voice.

'Oh there you are, where have you been? I've been worried sick! I was just about to phone the police. Of course you don't care about your old mother.'

Sarah kicked herself for not having contacted her sooner. Naturally her mother would have been worried, reading that piece in the paper, why hadn't she thought? She had just been busy, she was going to regret that for some time.

When they met at seven he asked where they were going.

'The Capital Gallery.'

'Oh very fancy!'

'I've got two tickets, a friend of mine gave them to me, to Nadir's latest exhibition preview.'

'Oh my God!'

'What's the matter?'

'Nothing, I'm not so keen on some modern art!'

'Nadir is the most important artist at the moment. His latest work, "Human Head in Aspic" is, well, really something. In fact this exhibition is titled, "Aspics of Taste".'

Brandon kept quiet. She prattled on.

'I was just thinking, my mother phoned when I got back, she was worried when she read the newspaper and was moaning about me not ringing her, I should have I know but she's always telling me I ought to go out more and I don't know why I didn't say, "Well, you told me to get out more!"'

'I don't think it would have been a good idea.'

'No, perhaps you're right.'

It felt nice having an arm to hang on to as they drifted round the rooms. It was a glittering affair and they were both underdressed. It made it nicer in a way, they were more like a couple. She bought comfortable, expensive clothes and tended to wear the same things all the time. Having learned to place comfort first when selecting her wardrobe, if she found something suitable she liked while shopping she would buy several. Being single, she avoided many of these events even though she'd organised a few. Maybe now she could get properly into the flow of life. They could visit galleries, go to the theatre perhaps, a few restaurants, build up a small coterie of friends. In her mind a vast horizon was opening up. This was the sort of change she wanted. Brandon kept making comments about the artist's work. A lot of them were amusing but they were also very unkind and Sarah wasn't sure how to take them.

Nudging him suddenly, Sarah whispered in his ear, 'Oh look, here comes Nadir now!'

In his late twenties and full of confidence, an attractive girl on each arm, the artist was laughing with his companions as he crossed the floor nearby. Catching sight of Brandon he paused and looked again.

'Brandon? Is that you? Wow! Hey! Brandon Tagg! How are you, man? I haven't seen you in ages. How are you doing?'

'I didn't know you knew Nadir!' exclaimed Sarah.

'I'm fine Jack, how are you?'

'Hey, this man always calls me Jack, like he's the *only* man who knows my real name. Hey girls, let me introduce you, this is Brandon. We go way back, we were at college together. This man is the best. He knocked the spots off all of us in our year, just bursting with ideas all the time. Gave it all up to go travelling, *had a vision*. Hey, man, you had some outlook! The whole world in your palm and you give it up to go travelling. What you doing now?'

'Still travelling!' Brandon answered without a moment's hesitation.

Sarah's jaw dropped in even deeper amazement.

'Hey that's crazy. I bet you got some stories!'

Nadir could remember their time in college distinctly. Brandon had always been the centre of attention. He had been quick and clever and everything he did won praise. While he laboured over one project, Brandon finished ten. Now the tables were turned. Now he'd made it, he had his picture in all the magazines, had put up a major exhibition and Brandon had practically disappeared. Who talked about Brandon Tagg now? Nobody, he'd dropped right out of the art world altogether. There was nothing he could say that would make the moment more perfect.

'Hey girls, this man!'

Words failed him briefly, he stood shaking his head as if he couldn't believe his eyes. His shaved head seemed to accentuate his large features, his big brown eyes and large nose. The girls didn't seem too impressed with Brandon and one of them kept asking if there was any more champagne, not that she needed any more. A large man in a dinner jacket bustled toward them through the throng, calling out as he approached.

'Nadir, please darling, come and meet Mr Lovelace, he's just back from Paris and is dying to see you and talk about your latest work.'

Having someone mention that one of the biggest patrons in the art world wanted to talk to him was an unlooked-for bonus.

'Hey look, Brandon, I gotta go, this man buys big. If you're in town why don't you come round sometime, catch up? It'd be great to talk. Anyway, catch you later.'

With that he followed the dinner jacket through the crowds. As soon as he had gone Sarah was clamouring excitedly.

'Was that true what he said that you were at college together? So did you study art? Why didn't you say anything before? Wow I can't get over this! I can't believe that you know Nadir! He's such a big name these days.'

'Yeah, I could see you having orgasms all over the place.'

'Don't be so disgusting! Why do you have to be so crude? And anyway, what do you mean?'

'You're just a glory hunter!'

'I beg your pardon, what?'

She was astonished.

'I'm sorry, I don't mean to be nasty, to spoil your evening, but I'm bound to just by being here. It would probably be best if I went.'

He made as if to go.

'No! You can't just leave me!'

'No, no of course I can't, I'm sorry.' He rubbed the back of his neck as if to relieve tension and then massaged his forehead.

Looking at her he said, 'The trouble is we're complete opposites, we've got completely different viewpoints.'

Unsure what to make of him, he obviously wasn't pleased about meeting with Nadir, she continued hanging on to him as they progressed round the exhibition. She saw and spoke to a few acquaintances as they passed but had no idea what she said to them.

'Why did you say you were still travelling?'

'I am!'

She looked at him uncomprehendingly. He tried to explain.

'Travelling is a state of mind. A lot of people will tell you they've been all over the world but you can tell they never see anything, they're no richer for it. It's not travel that enriches people, it's seeing things and learning from them. I see lots of things everywhere I go.'

'Why give up?'

'Who said I did?'

'But if what Nadir said is true you could have been somebody. I mean, he's huge right now and he said you knocked spots off them in college!'

'I am somebody!'

'But why drive buses?'

'It sounds like you think driving buses is a worthless occupation. In fact buses provide an important service people want.'

'Of course I don't denigrate bus drivers, it's just that you could do so much more.'

'There you are you see, "You could do so much more,"!'

'No, I mean it's just a different thing. Not everybody can be an artist. I mean if you're so good, it's such a waste. I don't understand!'

He turned on her and said, 'If you had all the people who chase after talent leaning over your shoulder all the time you *would* understand. So desperate for you to achieve so they can benefit it's obscene. So desperate some, they'll whip your work from you before it's dry just to prove they know you. They want your talent, they want your glory but most of all they're jealous of your life. If only they had your life they would live it *oh so* much better than you do. They would never stop creating brilliant things and they would never sleep. And the sad thing is that all the time they are wasting their own lives because they've missed the point. Social acclaim isn't what art is about. It's a process, you get involved and you never stop learning. My talent is mine, it's not for others to tell me how to use it. Everybody has a talent, something special they can do, it may not be conspicuous but it's there somewhere and should not be neglected. And these people insult God by ignoring their own gifts and insult you by telling you how to use yours. And if you had all these empty people clambering over your back, desperate for attention, you really would understand.'

He wasn't shouting but his voice had risen slightly as he said all this. It was enough for people to notice and when he finished Sarah was aware of a silent circle of eyes staring at them.

Embarrassed and upset, Sarah almost shouted herself, 'You shouldn't have come if you wanted to spoil everything. I just wanted this evening to be nice,' and, bashing him as hard as she could, she fled from the function.

That night her mind was like a whirlpool going round and dragging everything down. Why couldn't he have just been a nice quiet man? Why did he have to go and spoil everything opening his mouth like that? Why hadn't he said he knew Nadir or that he had studied art? Why did he hate Nadir? He must be jealous, Nadir was successful and he wasn't. She knew he wasn't jealous though, so that was wrong. It was something else. Why did she always meet such jagged people? Her whole life was so depressing. She had nobody to turn to. If she were to phone any of her friends they would ignore her problems and straightaway bombard her with their trivial events. They were married and much more important than she was. If she were robbed, raped and left for dead it wouldn't be as important as their husbands' comments at breakfast. Desperately wanting somebody to talk to, she had never felt so empty and lonely. Her only consolation was James and he didn't care at all. His new trick was to dash round the apartment and then hurl himself straight up her nicest drapes although once he was at the top of these he never seemed to be quite sure why. She did her best to train him out of it.

The clocks in the morning told her she must have slept. It hadn't made anything any better and she was still feeling guilty and very sorry for herself. Whatever he had said she shouldn't have run out like that. After saying he couldn't leave her she had left him! By way of a gesture she wrote an apologetic note with an invitation to coffee. She knew it wasn't the best offer in the world but if he had a heart he would at least be civil. Venturing upstairs, she was just going to slip the note under his door when it opened. She looked up at him. His face looked as haggard as she felt. Her voice sounded high and faint.

'We need to talk. Do you fancy a coffee?'

'I was just about to go out.' Reading her disappointment he said, 'Come with me if you want!'

'Okay, that would be good, I'll get my coat.'

Relief flooded through her.

'I'll treat you to a coffee later.'

He would never know how happy she was to hear that.

'That'll be great!'

As they set off he started to apologise,

'I'm sorry about last night . . .'

'No, it's me who should say I'm sorry!'

'Don't be silly!' he said.

This stopped them saying anything for ages but Sarah didn't mind at all. It was a gloomy day with low clouds too busy chasing each other round the tops of buildings to deliver rain. Eventually he started to talk.

'One of the reasons I drive a bus, or used to, is that nobody expects anything more than the job of me. When I was at college and even before that it always seemed the people around me always had to make me and whatever I did the centre of attention. I hated it. I don't know if I really did have good ideas or what but everybody made a fuss. Everybody waiting for fresh evidence. And even if I didn't put any effort into it it would be raved about. I could spill ink over a canvas and people would go into raptures. There was so much pretence. I just got sick of it.'

'But that's the price you have to pay for being good! Everybody loves success and it's natural for people to want to be near. Other people are successful, it doesn't bother them, I don't really understand your problem.'

'But the people that clamour to get in your limelight, most of them are just half people.'

'What do you mean?'

'Well, what I was saying last night, about people who don't know what to do with their lives, who don't know what they're good at and they try and muscle in on other people's action. Try and shine in other people's glory.'

'There are those sort of people everywhere, in all walks of life, you can't change them!'

'But the very nature of the subject I deal with is that it does change you, that's the whole point. Something really good changes you, adds something so you see the world a bit differently. And these people never change, they never grow, experience to them is just gaining street cred counters to display at the latest wild party.'

'I don't see why it matters to you so much.'

'Do you know any musicians?'

'What's that got to do with it?'

'Do you?'

'No!'

'Well, I've met and talked to quite a few over the years and I've noticed a lot of them have said the same thing.'

'What's that?'

'They could play the same piece of music at different places and it would sound completely different each time!'

'So?'

'The audience makes the difference!'

'I don't see your point.'

'The people who are paying attention have an effect on the performance. I think that audiences have an influence on art and when audiences are mainly composed of half-sighted, unfulfilled, self-serving, social climbers then art is bound to deteriorate. I think it has been deteriorating for a long time. Most art these days is just idealism and nasty idealism at that. It bears no relation to the original all around us.'

'Oh!'

'Sorry!' They walked in silence for a while as she digested what he had said.

'Are you going to go and see Nadir?'

'Heavens no, we hated each other at college, he was only being diplomatic last night because he thinks he's successful and I'm a failure. He just wants to gloat, not out loud of course but that's what he wants.'

'Why didn't you like each other?'

'Heaven knows. Why does anybody dislike somebody else? I don't know. I found him very pretentious. He used to idolise Warhol and I think he fancied himself as being as good as him. Only Warhol was very sensitive and produced some amazing drawings early on before he got into prints and things. Nadir can hardly draw at all, he runs off a few prints and thinks he's one of the greatest American artists. I just don't like that sort of thing.'

Happy the talk was easy, Sarah was conscious that nearly all he said demanded adjustments of her. She had always thought Nadir was good, now she had doubts. Each time they met she ended up having a lot of thinking to do. The next minute he had stopped and had pulled out a pad from an inside pocket of his raincoat. She had to wait while he made a note of a forest of signs she hadn't noticed were in the road before them. He contrasted these with the three sad trees on the corner of the small plot behind. It was exciting to be exploring the streets with him. She could see that some aspects of the places invigorated him and agreed that some things he pointed out were interesting. They walked down streets unknown to her and she realised they were getting into the rougher areas. At first she had been happy but now began expressing concern.

'Don't worry, we won't get any trouble, I've been round here several times before! I love the brooding blocks, there's a real atmosphere here!'

'Yeah, a scary one!' she said. 'Let's get back.'

'Okay,' he agreed, 'We'll just go down here.' He went across the street. By the side was what Sarah would only have described as junk. It had been a useful part of something once but now was a bent piece of metal. He lifted it up and looked at it from all angles before dropping it back in the gutter.

'Oh is this what you have in those boxes and bags that you are always carrying?' He nodded. 'What do you do with it?'

'I just use it. I get ideas when I see something sometimes. It doesn't always work. Not that it matters if it doesn't as it's only my time and effort wasted. Even then it's not wasted because I learn things. Sometimes they work very well, beyond my expectations and then it's really good. It's a real high.'

The hold-up was so quick and she was so scared and, although it happened right in front of her, she could never remember how he had talked his way out of it. Unbelievably, a short time later he was sat down drawing his attackers who were now all smiles. Brandon was obviously fascinated by their details and devoted a great deal of effort to execute them exactly. In the 20 minutes or so it took him to draw what she could see was a fine drawing a group of passers by and young children collected around him and watched him work. For the kids he pulled paper from the back of his pad and pencils from a pocket and told them to draw something particular for him. They happily got on, each intent on their own project. As she watched them, a feeling of pride emerging from the fright and turmoil inside her, a small boy asked if she would help him. Brandon had a sharpener and gave it when she asked.

'Of course, here, let me see,' and she knelt down beside the child and did some sharpening and then helped him with his picture. She could only wonder at herself who'd had no training either in teaching or art and yet was giving encouragement and instruction to a street urchin. Watching the struggling youngster beside her, she wanted to hold and protect him and stood up quickly to displace this urge.

Once he had finished Brandon stood up stiffly and swung one of his legs to regain feeling and restore the blood supply. The thieves, happy with their drawing which they could exchange for real money if they wanted to at an address Brandon wrote on the reverse, went off smiling. Them gone, Brandon sat down again and drew another sketch straight away from memory. Sarah was amazed how he could produce what looked to her an almost exact copy just out of his head.

'I like to be quick so I remember more details,' he explained.

When he'd done they had been standing and sitting for nearly an hour and by the time the children had been dealt with were both ready for a warm cafe and a cup of coffee. They set off to find one.

'Are you okay?' he asked.

She looked pale and cold as they sat down in the first cafe they could find and his voice was suddenly gentle and concerned.

'Yeah, I was just scared for a while.'

'Sorry!'

'You handled it so smoothly!'

'I've been lucky, art is a good equaliser. I mean

there is not much lower than a thief but they don't have any self-respect. Drawing people really gives them a boost.'

'And those kids, they would have done anything for you!'

'They don't have much and nobody gives them anything, least of all time.'

'I would never have given them a second glance before today and that one little boy wanted me, me of all people, to help him. And he was so intent on what he was doing it didn't matter we were by the side of the street, I couldn't believe it!'

The coffee came and he asked if she wanted a pastry or something to eat. He was hungry and she realised she was too.

Once the waitress had left them he continued, 'You need to cross boundaries,' he said grinning at her, his lively, dark grey eyes searching hers, 'It's all part of travelling!'

'You and your travelling!'

'It's not me, it's the universal preoccupation! Everybody zooming about in their cars, whizzing round the globe in planes.'

'But generally when people talk about travelling they mean seeing famous places for themselves instead of in books and on television, seeing different cultures and how other people live.'

'I know, Pyramids, Taj Mahal, people in poor countries. There is so much credence given to going to places like that. What about the streets we went down today, had you been there before?'

'No.'

'So what's the difference between them and the Pyramids?'

'Oh come on! They don't compare. You can't say

103

going out and about in the neighbourhoods broadens the mind.'

'The only thing that broadens the mind is stretching it to fit your body. Once you know your limits, then you've got a broad mind.' He continued, 'Who you're with matters as well. I remember meeting a refugee girl down by the waterfront who was perched on the top of a car feeding her baby. I just had to draw her and she didn't seem to mind. She was lonely and looked like she'd been crying. She was sitting up there in the wind feeding her baby in full view of the ocean so that her husband, who was still in Europe, would know they were there and come quickly. As if she and her love could be some sort of beacon to guide him. She was very beautiful, I must have spent an hour or so talking to her. She had travelled halfway round the world but none of the sights meant anything to her without her man. The wrong people distract you from the world and it takes the right people to open it up for you.'

He stacked his crockery and wiped his mouth with the napkin.

'Anyway, have you finished?'

'Here,' she said, 'lean forward!'

She couldn't help tidying his hair for him before stacking her crockery too. They left the cafe and started back home. Brandon began again.

'Art is always a two-way process, it's dynamic, there's a flow between yourself and your subject, between you and your material. It's the same if you really see something, it reaches inside and shakes you right up. I don't know how to describe it properly, it's an exchange I suppose. That's why I hate all these previews and things because it is always and necessarily a personal experience and not social. And you know that ninety nine per cent of the people who go to these things have never had such an experience or if they have it was so long ago it has been buried under gallons of champagne and platitudes.'

'I guess I can understand you wouldn't like them. I've always gone along with everything without really thinking. Then again, you're never going to change it all, the system's too big. I mean, you can't take on the world single-handed can you?'

'I've been lucky so far, pleasing myself what I do.'

'So you haven't given up then but how do you sell anything?'

'I don't.'

'So how do you manage?'

'Same as everybody else, I work.'

'Oh yes of course, I can't get over how you'd rather drive a bus than put your stuff on the market.'

'I've managed so far.'

'How do you find enough time to do everything?'

'I don't have enough time.'

'But if you didn't go to work maybe you would have.'

'Maybe. It doesn't always work out. I've known people with all the time in the world end up doing nothing.'

Sarah knew this was true. She remembered Michael had spent days doing nothing when he'd given up and if he'd only had the will he could easily have been out working. She had been frustrated with his inability to get a grip on things but now she knew he probably had some depressive disorder and should have had treatment of some sort. Life is all very well in hindsight.

'I don't know, maybe I'll change. I'm giving it a lot of thought at the moment,' Brandon declared.

They passed a paper kiosk and bought the Sunday papers to read.

'Hey, we're doing this the wrong way round,' she said. 'We should have read the papers this morning!'

'Yeah, I know, but I needed a walk.'

'So did I. Look, I could make some lunch if you fancy coming back to mine.'

Brandon readily agreed. Cooking wasn't his favourite occupation. When they got in James took to him straight away and kept climbing his trousers while Brandon tried to keep him down.

'Jeez, he's got sharp claws!' Brandon exclaimed.

'Don't I know!'

Sarah was pleased to be cooking for somebody and quickly made some pasta. She had to act casual putting it on the table. Brandon was impressed with her meal and ate a lot. After dinner they spent a quiet afternoon each reading their papers.

'It says here there was a big celebratory event for the Bashfords last night. Apparently your boss's family have put all their money into setting up a foundation to look after Third World children. I bet he's happy about that!'

'Yeah, I know. A friend of mine's husband was involved in arranging the finances to set up the foundation. Poor Mr Bashford had been in a funny mood for a couple of weeks before he disappeared. Mind you it's not often he's in anything else. Still he shouldn't have just left us without any warning whatsoever.'

'You said he had a lot of good qualities!'

'Well, I don't know, he pays a decent salary and lets me get on with it. Just because he's moody doesn't mean he's bad.'

There was more. Teller had written an amusing article about the plight of the city galleries. He had noticed a number of anomalies which in the current climate were puzzling. He wondered if any of the authorities were curious, or not for any particular reason. Most likely it was just coincidence that these disparities were overlooked and the revenue not needed anyway. Also, commenting on the trade of ancient artifacts that was despoiling the Third World of its heritage and lining the pockets of thieves, he was glad that in such and open and caring business as theirs none of the city galleries would stoop that low.

'Hey look, read this, this is what you were saying the other day. Did you know about this?' she asked him.

'Yes, Teller came to see me the other night.'

'I saw him! He was here! Oh! He came here? You know Teller! How do you know him?'

'I met him at college, he was at some sort of do they had once and we just hit it off, he's a really nice bloke.'

'You know everybody!'

'Far from it!'

'I'm beginning to understand now. It's no wonder Mr Bashford disappeared, he's been having a hard time lately, what with his parents and this!'

'Teller has generally got his finger on the pulse. He has an amazing mind.'

'It explains all the phone calls we had on Friday. I was so embarrassed. You feel so stupid with people ringing up all the time and you don't know what's going on. You can even feel them thinking at the other end that you must be really dim and can't know your job and it's not true at all. We were kept in the dark.'

'Well, it's not the sort of thing they would tell you about, is it?'

'I suppose not. What do you think will happen?'

'I shouldn't think anything will happen.'

'But these things are awful.'

'People in the highest position in the land have done far worse things and got away with it. I should think they'll just sit tight and bluff it out. Business will go down for a while so they might take long holidays but they'll just carry on. The only time things will change is if these people develop honesty.'

'What if I end up losing my job?'

'I doubt if you would but I'm sure Teller would employ you.'

'Do you think so?'

'I'm certain of it.'

Turning a new page, Brandon suddenly groaned.

'Oh no, what's this? Oh no, I could have done without this!'

'What's the matter?'

He showed her the page. Under a lurid headline there was a photo of them taken at the preview.

'I didn't see anybody take that!' exclaimed Sarah.

Brandon read the text.

'"Seen here for the first time in many years our photographer spotted Brandon Tagg, here talking to his host at Nadir's hugely successful preview, see main article. It is rumoured that there will be another preview soon when Brandon opens his own exhibition. The young prodigy who dropped out of his final year of college to pursue a career in the travel industry is believed to be ready to open an exhibition, we can't say yet if it will be, 'Going Anywhere.' Perhaps he was asking Nadir for some advice! We wait with bated breath."'

'Oh Jeez, I don't know where they get all this stuff from. Anyway it isn't true because I finished my course, I didn't drop out at all. These people have no idea what the truth is when they write. I'm gonna have to make some phone calls. I'll have to get back.'

108

Sarah was still reading the article.

'It says here you might be having an exhibition, is that right?'

'Maybe, it's not settled yet. I'd like to know how these people got wind of it, I certainly haven't told anybody.'

'You're hoping to have an exhibition of your work?'

'If it all goes through.'

'Why didn't you tell me?'

'Because it's not finalised.'

'I don't know what to say, every minute you've got some new revelation you can't be bothered to tell me about! Where is it going to be?'

'At the Teller Gallery.'

'Well it pays to have friends in high places.'

'I'm sorry, I should have said I suppose. It's habit keeping everything to myself and all this has happened so fast.'

'Is it what you want?'

'I don't know. It's tearing me apart. I've been thinking about it all the time recently. I've had an idea for something I want to put together, a sort of experiment. The thing is I can't win. On the one hand I am quite excited about it. On the other hand I've always hated exhibitions. It's only now I've thought of something I want to do with one. I've been talking with Teller and he thinks the time is right and is giving me the backing. We'll see if it all works out. I don't know. I'm not sure.' He paused, 'Did you hear about the indecisive scatologist?'

'No!' she yelled and made to cover her ears with cushions.

'He fell between two stools.'

He grinned as she threw the cushions at him.

'Anyway I have to shoot off now, I'll see you later!'

109

She wasn't sure if he meant he would be back later that evening or what. She hoped he would be back and waited up for him just in case but he didn't appear.

That night she had one of the most vivid dreams ever. It was in a massive terminus building. There were corridors and passages leading off everywhere and she seemed to be traipsing through every one. She was in the middle of the complicated process of changing trains. The train she needed to catch was right on the other side of the building and it meant going down to get across. Speed was vital, the trains were due to leave. She could take the elevator down, which meant walking miles, or jump. As she was struggling to make this decision she suddenly knew all the trains had departed. Her train had gone without her. It didn't seem to matter too much because then she was swimming. Gliding through this building which it seemed was a giant pool and not a terminus and all the tunnels were pretty caves with jewels. It was lovely and everything was bright and crystal clear. A long time passed as she swam before it occurred to her she was breathing the water. That was impossible and it was important she get up to the surface and take a breath of air. The surface was a long way up. It was beginning to be a struggle. Then she woke up, hot and bothered.

The alarm had gone off over an hour ago. There was no memory of hearing it at all although she must have turned it off. After a much needed shower she made some coffee and tried to get her head round the simple task of getting dressed. Her head was still swimming and no matter how much she urged herself she could not rush. In the end she decided that she was late anyway and might as well have a decent breakfast, take

110

her time and get sorted. She phoned in and told them at work she would be late. Looking from her window as she phoned, she could see it was a bright day with hardly any clouds, just the trails of jets across the edges. Outside she found it was definitely a bit warmer. Perhaps this was proof the long winter was on its way out. It was nice being late as the subway was empty and there was a choice of seats. If she ever won the lottery, giving up the rush hour would certainly be worth considering.

When she arrived at work Mr Bashford was in the foyer.

She was sure he didn't recognise her for he made as if to greet a visitor but when she said, 'Hello Mr Bashford,' he turned back mumbling, 'Oh it's you, Sarah, you've cut your hair!' Then turning on her again he demanded,

'Where have you been? You should have been here two hours ago, it's nearly eleven.'

'I'm sorry,' she said, not caring at all, 'I overslept.'

'Well, it's not good enough, I'll overlook it this time but you'll please be more punctual in future!' and he left her to go to his office.

She was a bit taken aback by this. In all her seven years she had never once been late or even had time off sick. After all the trials of the last week, working hard without any support and without knowing what was going on and now he couldn't even be bothered to thank her for keeping everything running. He couldn't treat her like that and moan now. Surprising herself, she made a decision. Leaving her coat on she sat down at her desk and wrote a letter of resignation. She pinched a box from the store and collected up her belongings. Having nearly three weeks holiday owing to her anyway, she saw no reason to stay there a moment longer. She wished everybody good luck and promised to keep in touch.

When she was ready she walked straight into Mr Bashford's office, handed him the letter and said, 'Goodbye,' with such finality he was speechless.

On her way home she picked up some college prospectuses. In the back of her mind an idea was developing and she needed to find out how she could make it possible. As she travelled the rest of the way she noticed some blossom was out on a cherry tree. It was the first she had seen this year. At her apartment James was so pleased to see her it took her mind off having thrown away her job. Later on she tidied herself up and went up to see if Brandon was in and tell him the news. He was in and when she told him what she'd done he stood staring at her in amazement.

'That's incredible! That's exactly what I've done. Isn't that incredible! I'm on holiday anyway but I went in to the office earlier and gave my notice in. It's unbelievable we should both do exactly the same thing at exactly the same time.'

'I didn't realise you were serious about giving up your job. I know you talked about it but I didn't know you'd do it definitely.'

Now she felt unhappy about her spontaneous decision. Having been careful all her life, she didn't like uncertainty. This was change a bit too far, especially if Brandon was equally reckless.

'No I didn't either. I don't know if it's this thing next door. Both of them were only young. Life is so short anyway and you never know what might happen. Only I was doing some work last night and it struck me that I've got so much to do. It's funny we were talking about it the other day. I've been all right so far just plodding along but now all of a sudden I've got a

112

million and one more ideas. It's like my brain's gone into hyperdrive! I know I need a lot more time to get on with it. If I'm to do it properly I can't keep the job as well. It must be all the celery!' he added, giving her a grin.

As he looked at her he saw her expression.

'What's the matter?' he asked.

He seemed to sense her anxieties.

'I don't know. Giving up my job was a snap decision and I'm not really prepared. For a few minutes when I did it I had a clear picture of how things would work out but in reality nothing is so simple. I've given up my job, what am I going to do?'

'As I said yesterday, Teller will give you a job.'

'How can you say that?'

'I'm sure he will!'

'Well, I don't know.' She was doubtful and didn't trust his confidence. 'Have you got any coffee? I could do with some.'

'Most definitely, there's some cake left too if you want it!'

While he made the coffee she sat watching him.

'It was quite an eventful day yesterday. It could have been horrible but it wasn't,' she admitted.

'Yeah, it was nice, nice to have company!'

'You didn't come back, I wasn't sure if you were going to come back.'

'Oh I'm sorry, I was down at the studio, I got completely engrossed in what I was doing. I didn't think you were expecting me. I am sorry.'

'Doesn't matter,' she said. 'I had a really vivid dream last night!' and she went on to describe it.

'Dreams are weird,' he said, 'I can never make them out. When you're having them they make complete sense but when you wake up they're just too fantastic.'

'I know.'

'One thing I've noticed, I've never dreamt about driving! I've driven thousands of miles each year and I've never had one dream about it. Isn't that strange?'

'I guess it isn't important to you, you never talk about your driving. Anyway you won't be doing it any more now so I don't suppose you will dream about it.'

'Yeah, could be. Either that or I'll have a million dreams about driving now.'

A bit later after coffee and cake Sarah returned to her own apartment. There were several things she had to do, one of which was phoning her mother with her news. She thought it was not likely to be well received. Having talked to Brandon about it she felt happier and a bit more optimistic. She had some money put by and if she could study she might be eligible for a grant or something. Brandon said he had to take some stuff down to the studio but would be back in a hour or so and he invited her round, offering to cook in return for her meal yesterday. When he came back he found the detectives had turned up to ask a few questions.

'Okay, come in,' he invited.

They made themselves at home, looking in the room Brandon usually kept people out of. Nosing about, Cheapowski began to touch things here and there. An overweight, middle-aged balding detective, he had a round face, moustache and beady eyes and what dark hair he had left straddled his collar.

'What were you doing last Thursday night?'

'I can't remember.'

'That's convenient. What is this crap?'

'Don't touch that, it's important!'

'What is it?'

'Something I'm working on.'

114

'So, some sort of hobby sticking bits of tin can together?'

'That's exactly it. However, I'd rather you didn't touch it. It's valuable to me!'

'For a coach driver you've got a high opinion about tin cans!'

'Not nearly as high as yours about yourself!'

'So how does being a coach driver give you such attitude?'

'The world's a sad place when people have to answer to unimaginative scatologists.'

'What's this scatologist crap?'

'A scatologist is somebody who studies faeces.'

'What are you saying?' The angry detective raised his finger, pointing at Brandon, 'Listen, pal, I work hard to make the place safe for ordinary people, people like you!'

'Yeah, so you can insult them in their own homes!'

At that moment there was a knock on the door. Brandon went and opened it letting Teller in.

'Are you all right Brandon? I heard there's been some sort of violence.'

'Yeah, I'm all right, all that was the other night, next door. I've just got some detectives with me now.'

He raised his eyes heavenward in disgust. The newcomer and detective exchanged greetings.

'And you are?' the detective enquired.

'William Teller, a friend.'

'Just out of curiosity, Mr Teller, can you see anything in this pile of tin cans?'

'This? This is upside down at the moment. I'm hoping to acquire this myself. I have a reasonable collection already but I like these things very much. I have it insured for fifty thousand so be careful!'

115

The detective turned sharply, knocking the object under discussion which wobbled but fortunately didn't topple.

'Are you shitting me? Are you trying to say this is worth something, that it's "Art" or something?'

'I like it, I don't care what people call it.'

'If you say it's worth all that money, how come you can afford it?'

'Perhaps you have heard of the Teller Corporation?'

'That's you?'

Cheapowski was surprised.

'That's me!'

'What are you doing in a place like this?'

'Jesus!' Brandon exploded, 'Actually, if you've got time, detective, I'd like to show you something. If you could give me a hand, William,' he went over and indicated his intention.

'Turn it over, sure,' Teller complied.

They very gingerly lifted the thing, which was quite heavy, turned it and set it down again. It was a great, crimson globe on a thick, dark green shaft. The detective wasn't impressed and asked,

'What am I looking at?'

Brandon plugged it in and threw a switch at the back and then went and pulled the blinds shut. They were all stood in the dark now.

'There's a fifteen second delay,' explained Brandon as nothing happened.

Then very faintly at first the bud began to glow and ever so gently began to burst and unwrap and growing brighter all the time as delicate petals slowly spread from the centre and a strong scent of roses filled the room. Once fully open, the golden pink rose paused in all its glory for a minute before its light died and it snapped shut. Brandon pulled the blinds open again.

'I ain't never seen anything like that! No, sir, I ain't never seen anything like that!'

Cheerful actually spoke.

'Say, that was good,' Cheapowski admitted, 'That must have taken some work. See, I can appreciate that, a lot of stuff these days has got nothing to it but that, you can see that!'

'I think you had the wrong impression,' observed Brandon.

'Maybe I did, maybe I did.'

'Anyway,' Teller began, 'if you have no more questions then perhaps you'd leave us. I have some important business to discuss with Mr Tagg and my time is valuable.'

Brandon, nearer the door, opened it to allow the detectives to leave. Outside was Sarah just about to knock.

'Oh . . .' she said, startled.

The detective eyed her suspiciously.

'You're another friend?'

'Yes, you've spoken to me before, I live downstairs, directly below,' Sarah answered.

The detective turned back to Brandon and asked his question again.

'So you can't remember where you were on Thursday night last week?'

'No I can't remember,' Brandon replied.

Sarah spoke up, 'It's all right, Brandon. I can tell you, detective, Brandon was with me that evening.'

'He was with you? Where?'

'Here.'

'Thank you, detectives, is that all?' asked Teller firmly.

He drew Sarah in around the policemen and closed the door as they left.

'Good afternoon,' he said to Sarah, 'I believe we've met before. I didn't realise you were a friend of Brandon's. Brandon, you should have told me you had a spy in the enemy camp!'

Teller winked at her. He was very pleased to see Sarah. He had known young Brandon for several years now, supporting him one way or another since the boy had turned his back on the mainstream. He'd given him his first job as his chauffeur, paying him too much and asking very little of him, preferring to take taxis rather than disturb his drawing. Brandon was always drawing something. He had encouraged him when he wanted to move on and had always kept in touch. In all that time he'd never seen him with company. Teller had been blessed with a long and happy marriage and was glad to see Brandon with a lady friend. He would have liked everybody to have been as lucky as he himself was.

'Enemy camp, what do you mean?' Sarah asked.

'Do you mind if I have a brief, private word with Brandon, I won't be long then he'll be all yours as I have to go. I have an important meeting to get to, in fact I should be there already.'

'No, not at all, go ahead!'

As the two walked toward the kitchen Brandon thought of one of his jokes.

'Hey, what does a scatologist do for entertainment?'

She didn't hear the punchline but judging by Teller's laughter he had the same sense of humour as Brandon. Sarah smiled and entered the room she'd not seen before. It smelt nice. In her apartment it was the living room but for Brandon it was a store cupboard that was crammed full of his work. In most of the wall space were hung huge paintings and there were more paintings stacked on the floor. There were shelves loaded with sculptures. In the middle of the room was a work table and the only other item of furniture was a very old and tatty leather armchair. At the other end were maybe 20 portfolios which she guessed contained drawings like the ones he'd made on their walk. She went to investigate, opening one and looking through the drawings in it and then opening another to do the same. She had been right, each one was packed with a fantastic variety of drawings. There were portraits galore, some were delicate outlines, some quick sketches, others were intense, heavily worked studies. The wealth of material amazed her. So absorbed in it all she didn't hear Teller shout, 'Goodbye!' and when Brandon came in she was holding in her hand a picture of a tear-streaked mother and child.

Sensing him near she looked up and said, 'This is beautiful!'

'How would you know?'

'I beg your pardon?'

Her generally upright posture slumped a little as she looked at him unbelievingly.

'You know I'm interested in beautiful things, I'm always . . .'

'No! You only see beauty where you've been told to. Once somebody has put a frame round it, then you see it. But that isn't beauty, the real beauty is all around us, naked, without a frame! This isn't beauty, this is my poor attempt to clutch it, to hold it in my hands for a few desperate moments before my eyes cloud over. You think this is beauty, you're living second-hand!'

With this on top of the events of the last few days Sarah was suddenly overwhelmed and she sat down on the arm of the chair and buried her face in her hands. Shocked by her silent sobbing, Brandon felt guilty and stupid.

'I'm sorry,' he said, and then, 'You shouldn't have lied to the police! They'll only find out. They're bound to get whoever did it in the end.' She looked up at him and her face, completely crumpled under his apparent rejection, tore his heart to pieces.

'Hey, hey, hey, I'm sorry, I'm sorry.'

Putting his arms around her, he patted and stroked her as she sobbed into his shoulder.

'What you did was the nicest thing anybody has ever done for me. I'm sorry, I didn't mean to hurt you. Nobody has ever done anything like that for me before,' and he rocked her comfortingly.

After a while she quieted and they realised everything had changed. He reached down and picked up the drawing she'd let fall.

'This is that girl!' he exclaimed, 'The girl on the car. You know I was telling you. I did another picture of her, I made into a painting.'

He got up and started flicking through the canvases leaning against the wall, finally pulling out the one he was after.

'Here,' and he lifted it up for her to see.

'I think it's beau . . . lovely,' she said.

He looked at her and then put the painting down.

'I'm sorry. I shouldn't have said all that. I've wanted you for such a long time and this has all happened so quick. I've been alone so long, I'm not used to it. I'm sorry.'

'Don't keep saying you're sorry!'

As they touched, as she fell into his embrace, Time and the Universe were replaced by a new measure, a determination of warmth and sensation. There was nothing so correct as this kiss that ended all solitude. Trembling, their mouths caressing the sweetest taste of all that heated and stirred them both beyond return. As they made their way to the bedroom and their clothes fell, ten senses interlocked, tuned by the atomic calibration of skin. She had never known such gentle, tender comfort and sweetness as they settled into each other's arms touching everywhere possible. They seemed to glide together, thirsty rivers into the ocean that ebbed and flowed almost forever until the moon's tidal pull flooded them both with an ardent and urgent need. She had a split second of panic as she thought he was dying when at the pitch of a momentous lunge he gasped and slumped on her. For a moment she thought she was going too, was also about to die. Another moment and she didn't care as she notched herself into ecstasy around him. Resurfacing an eternity later, a twitching, soggy, tangle, a metallic taste and hollowness in her head and then the full heat returned and she clasped the snatching, the cold skinned and hot, hairy and sweat smelly body of flesh and limbs everywhere in her arms as tight, as tight as she possibly could to never let go of the lover that had electrified every single one of her nerves.

They lay, completely content, hardly talking, looking at each other for hours as darkness descended around them.

'You've never mentioned my scar,' she observed.

'Everybody has scars!' he said, dismissing it.

She sighed and said, 'I hardly know anybody in this building, I'm glad I met you.'

'You're not like that old biddy on the second floor.'

'Who, Maureen?'

'I don't know her name but I think she knows everybody in this building and their business. Sometimes the things I bring back or take out are too big to go in the elevator and I have to walk down the stairs and if I do you can bet your last dollar she's there peeping out from behind her door. I don't say anything apart from, "Hello." I can tell she's dying to know what I'm doing. Then again I could always tell you wanted to know what I was carrying. Remember when we first spoke?' he asked. 'I had that big box. I knew you were going to ask what it was. I wanted to tell you too but at the last minute I couldn't.'

'Well, like I said, I'm just nosy.'

'It's a good job you are or we never would have spoken.'

'It was James's fault. It was him that brought us together.'

'Getting that cat was a good idea!'

'I wish I'd got him sooner!'

Eventually she shoved him to turn on the light. He reached over and switched on the lamp. The bulb blew. He swore and got up, dragging a dressing gown round himself and went to switch the main light on. That bulb blew too. Swearing again, he left the room and returned with another lamp which he plugged in and successfully lit. He went back out leaving her for a while. She found him sitting in his dressing gown in the kitchen gazing vacantly out of the dark window.

'Are you all right?' she asked, scratching her head vigorously.

'Yeah,' he answered. 'Yeah, you know three light bulbs blew and two clocks have stopped.'

'That's a bit scary!'

'It is a bit.'

She made some tea and they went back to bed to drink it. He put some music on quiet and they listened without speaking.

'I thought of another joke,' he declared all of a sudden.

'Not another shit joke I hope.'

'What did the lovelorn scatologist find?' he asked regardless.

'I don't know, I hate these!' she exclaimed, rubbing her scalp again.

'He found, "Poetry in motions!"'

'You really are revolting!' she told him but he just laughed and laughed.

She knew it wasn't his joke but his happy mood and she caught the infection and ended up laughing too.

A little while later, when they had subsided and the music had finished, Sarah remembered her little kitten.

'Hey look, my hair is really itchy, I need to give it a wash and also to check on James, he'll be getting lonely. How about if I go down and I can cook something for us in my place. You could come down now or later if you want.'

In life we miss so much. Great chunks from even the most interesting of stories. We catch a glimpse every then and now. Our imagination helps us fill the gaps. For us, miraculously free from this hurly-burly, we can see the patterns in people's lives, their successes, their mistakes and failures. We know the fragile joys they have and their desperate desolation. We believe they are made for each other. We know his exhibition will change the world. We know the attention and hypocrisy will drive him away. We know she will study, take up teaching and also change the world and yet her patient heart will be waiting, unchanged, for his return. At the moment our lives aren't pressing all around us for answers but, having sat on the building for so long, we are getting numb. The events have been fascinating but we are drifting off. We never get the complete picture. As we go the world drops away from us. Even of our own world we only see one side. Beyond the weather we can see it turning, a bright blue jewel spinning in the emptiness. We pretend this view is our own but in the back of our minds we know it won't be long.